Teaching at the Top of the World

An adventurous woman's frightful and humorous tales—the characters she met, life on the Trans-Alaska pipeline, and teaching in Alaska Bush villages.

Marilyn Forrester

Since 1978

PO Box 221974 Anchorage, Alaska 99522-1974
books@publicationconsultants.com
www.publicationconsultants.com

ISBN 978-1-59433-162-6
ebook 978-1-59433-175-6
Library of Congress Catalog Card Number: 2010937304

Copyright 2010 Marilyn Forrester
—Second Edition—

Marilyn's website address is: www.marilynforrester.com

Marilyn's blog address is: www.marilynforrester.blogspot.com

All rights reserved, including the right of
reproduction in any form, or by any mechanical
or electronic means including photocopying or
recording, or by any information storage or
retrieval system, in whole or in part in any
form, and in any case not without the
written permission of the author and publisher.

Manufactured in the United States of America.

Dedication

This book is dedicated to two remarkable women, my sisters Pat Philip and Hazel Mills, with my deepest appreciation for the constancy of their love, loyalty, and unceasing encouragement.

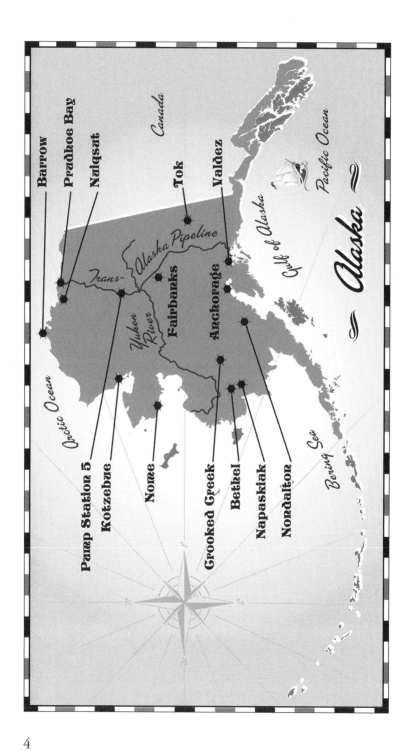

Barrow
Prudhoe Bay
Nuiqsut
Tok
Valdez
Canada
Pacific Ocean
Alaska Pipeline
Trans-
Fairbanks
Anchorage
Gulf of Alaska
Yukon River
Arctic Ocean
Pump Station 5
Kotzebue
Nome
Crooked Creek
Bethel
Napaskiak
Nondalton
Bering Sea
Alaska

Author's Disclaimer

Author's Disclaimer: This book is based on my experiences as a teacher in rural villages of Alaska. I lived in these villages many years ago and have been told that teacher housing, morale and conditions have improved. Names of characters have been changed out of courtesy and concern for the privacy of the people depicted. I am grateful for the experiences and friendships made during my teaching career and have the utmost respect for the people who have touched my life.

Acknowledgements

I want to take this opportunity to acknowledge the following people: Kathi-Jo Skaats and Betty Kelley, good friends and valued confidantes who always listened when I needed to talk, offered advice even when I didn't ask for it, and never failed to urge me forward as I wrote about my Alaska experience.

Special thanks to my two supporters, Kay Elliott and Penny Ramos, who assisted me with the editing of this book.

"If we could sell our experiences for
what they cost us, we'd be millionaires."
Abigail Van Buren

One

January, 1977

I was forty years old, just getting over a failed marriage and the subsequent divorce.

My father watched me pack my suitcase as he spoke. "I wish you were going anywhere in the world but that God forsaken place. Why Alaska?"

My hands rested on the sweater I'd just folded. "Instinct," I said, suddenly realizing the truth of my response. "Pure instinct."

"I hated it when you were wandering all over Europe. And then, of course, there was Israel," he recalled, shaking his head. "I'm worried you're making a mistake."

"Mom worries. You . . ." I began.

"I worry, too. Probably more than you realize." He studied me from beneath bushy brows. Of medium height, overweight, and gray haired, my Dad symbolized love and security to me.

"Trust me, Dad. I know what I'm doing."

He fingered the electric blanket atop my suitcase. "They probably don't even have electricity up there."

I smiled. I had a history of taking off to various places around the globe, but I always survived. "I'll be fine, Dad."

"What are you going to do once you get there?"

I grinned at him. "Get a job as a welder on the pipeline. Maybe even get rich."

He frowned. "You don't know anything about welding. Besides, the pipeline's almost finished."

I wasn't discouraged. I needed a change. More than a change, I realized, I needed and intended to have a bona fide adventure.

"You don't know a soul up there."

"I do know someone. He's an old friend, and he's going to put me up while I find a job and look for my own place."

"Is he reliable?"

I laughed. I couldn't help myself. "You're the only reliable man I've ever known, Dad."

"How are you fixed for money?" he pressed.

I thought about the $15 hamburgers my friend had mentioned. "All right, if things get tight, I'll become a vegetarian."

He glanced at my suitcase. "Maybe you should pack steaks instead of clothes."

I smiled as I closed the suitcase. His embrace brought stinging tears to my eyes.

I departed the next day and took $200, a return airline ticket, and enough dreams to fill another piece of luggage.

Two

Bob Wolfe met my flight at the Anchorage airport. He hadn't changed a bit. Tall, skinny, and big-nosed, he wore a huge parka and snow boots. After greeting me with an enthusiastic hug, he led me out to his Bronco and stowed my luggage.

I immediately realized that my winter clothes wouldn't even begin to protect me from the sub-zero Alaska temperatures. The need for employment and an income became even more acute.

As we drove to his house, Bob told me about his job flying up and down the pipeline for Xerox and installing machines at the different pump stations. He also rented rooms in his house to six men who came and went like the residents of a fraternity house. My temporary quarters belonged to a man currently enjoying a week long vacation. It finally occurred to me that Bob intended to resume our old affair, but that wasn't my plan.

By week's end, Bob's desire for me to move out was apparent. A telephone conversation that I overheard prompted me to intensify my efforts to find both a place to live and gainful employment.

I searched the city for inexpensive lodging, becoming a source of despair for several bus drivers, who often took pity on me and personally guided me to many of my destinations. Some of them probably regretted their kindness to me, but I will be forever grateful for their generosity and good-natured tolerance.

My search for a place to live resulted in Mrs. Legg. Her home was close to the center of town, and she was advertising for a boarder. The added bonus was her willingness to wait to be paid until I found a job. That sold me.

Bob helped me move my few possessions into Mrs. Legg's house. Although he politely urged me to stay in touch, I think he was relieved to be rid of me. I was more than glad to be out of the frat house.

Mrs. Legg, a dumpy little woman with straggly looking white hair that framed her face, suffered from emphysema. I must admit that she was kind at first, but I soon realized that Mrs. Legg needed a full-time nurse who would also pay rent.

Needless to say, our landlord-tenant relationship was fraught with all manner of conflicts and destined to fail.

Three

I spent all of my time looking for a job. Without a car, I walked several miles each day, when I didn't ride the various Anchorage buses. That didn't hurt my figure one bit, but who would ever notice since I was dressed for warmth and resembled a cumbersome Nanook of the North?

After contacting several potential employers, Alyeska Pipeline invited me for an interview. I dressed with care and arrived early for my appointment with Mr. Watson. My interview proved to be unconventional, however.

Mr. Watson, in charge of Surplus Management, oversaw the disposal of all assets from Pump Station Number 1 to the Valdez Terminal. An Ichabod Crane look-alike with red hair, Watson had just begun to question me about my qualifications for a secretarial position when the fire alarm blared. Everyone vacated the building in a scrambling rush.

Watson resumed the interview as we stood outside. Our teeth chattered and bodies shook from the bitter cold. I can't remember a single word of our exchange.

Once we returned to Watson's office, he shocked me by saying, "You've got the job. When can you start?"

I hadn't even taken a typing test. I was dumb-founded, but who was I to argue with my good fortune? I also concluded that the Alyeska Anchorage office must be desperate for secretaries. I wisely did not mention my goal to work as a welder on the pipeline or the paucity of my clerical skills. Sometimes, discretion is the better part of valor.

And, as far as I was concerned, eating on a regular basis definitely took precedence over adventure and my desire to make bucket-loads of money.

The State of Alaska mandated that only residents of Alaska could be hired for the job I'd just been employed to do at Alyeska. In order to circumvent this edict and gain hiring approval from the state, Watson supplied me with a document to present to the State Employment Office that verified no other qualified applicant could be found for the position. In return, the State of Alaska provided me with an identification card signed by the governor, which certified me as a legal resident of Alaska.

Only two weeks had passed since my arrival in Anchorage!

To celebrate my good fortune, I attended a singles party at the Unitarian Church, which I'd found advertised in the local paper. A member of the congregation even offered to pick me up and take me to the party that Saturday night.

True to form, Mrs. Legg expressed her displeasure about my social plans. She expected my company each evening. Sounding like a truculent child, she told me, "I'll leave the deadbolt unlocked. Don't wake me up when you get home."

Alice Cameron, a teacher, picked me up for the singles party. The man in her life, she explained without preamble, was a doctor. Her territorial tone of voice contained a clear 'hands off' warning. I took one look at her doctor, who appeared to be older than dirt and the possible victim of a severe case of rickets, and realized I wouldn't have wanted him even if he'd been the last of his gender on the planet.

Since shyness isn't my curse, I enjoyed the party. Everyone exclaimed over my adventurous spirit when they learned that I'd arrived in Alaska without the promise of employment. I met Bill Sampson that night. Already a practicing attorney in another state, he was studying for the Alaska bar exam.

Bill, a tall, attractive man, approached me. "How long will you be in Anchorage?"

I grinned, easily adopting the exaggeration impulse of all Alaskans. "I'm in transit to Israel, so I'll just be here for the weekend."

He looked startled, and I'm still convinced he thought I was a cryptic Jew. We soon drifted in opposite directions that night, and I didn't expect to see him again.

The next day I received a phone call from Bill. He'd gone to a great deal of trouble, telephoning several people and finally tracking me down at Mrs. Legg's home. You can imagine my surprise when he asked me out for the evening.

Before departing on my date, Mrs. Legg cautioned me not to go anywhere near Spenard or Mountain View. She counseled in a morose tone, "They're rough areas. Anything could happen to you there."

That was also when she told me about 'Spenard divorces'. In the past, Alaska had suffered from a severe shortage of women. If a woman shot her husband, she wouldn't be brought to trial, because Alaskan men weren't willing to forfeit even one available female.

Mrs. Legg's displeasure continued into the next morning. "If you're going to be out all night, at least be quiet when you come home."

I dated Bill for several months. Mrs. Legg turned nasty whenever I didn't arrive home by midnight. She'd secure the deadbolt when she went to bed, thus forcing me to ring the doorbell to gain entry into the house. I simmered with fury. Mrs. Legg became more and more intransigent. Our cold war persisted, neither one of us willing to back down. I often stayed at Bill's apartment; it was easier than ringing the doorbell in the middle of the night and dealing with my landlady.

In the meantime, I loved my job at Alyeska. One of my co-workers, April, a lanky blonde with huge brown eyes, was trapped in a miserable marriage to an engineer who worked for a competing oil company. A former Florida resident, April loathed Alaska.

Typically, most oil executive wives hated Alaska. They longed to return to their Lower Forty-Eight homes. They disliked the weather, the oppressive darkness, and the lack of decent shopping. They also missed their friends. Their husbands, on the other hand, thought they'd died and gone to heaven, especially since most of them hunted and fished. As well, most oil executives lived in upscale homes and made excellent money.

April and her husband lived in a lovely apartment not far from our office. She walked to work each day. We lunched together and watched out for one another professionally. Because April realized I hadn't brought much of a wardrobe with me to Alaska, she gave me first shot at her cast-off clothing before donating what I couldn't use to charity. I gratefully accepted, having no pride when it came to being warm and expanding my minimalist clothing selections.

April and I hit it off the instant we met. Unlike the other secretarial and clerical staff, we could spell correctly and construct complete sentences, and we both possessed the normal confidence of intelligent women.

The men in our department loved us. They even brought us gifts, but not because we were so good at our jobs. If anything, it was because the rest of the clerical staff was so bad. No one ever discovered April's habit of stuffing her purse with typo-filled pages. As far as everyone was concerned, perfection was April's middle name.

We enjoyed Alyeska. There were parties, inter-office intrigue, back stabbing, and a wealth of unfounded gossip. I also learned just how difficult it would be to obtain a job on the pipeline. Had I played Hollywood starlet and slept with the men responsible for staffing the pump stations, I probably would have been much more successful in my quest.

Mrs. Legg grew more and more difficult. The cold war escalated to open warfare. I worried constantly about being locked out of the house in the middle of the night. Mrs. Legg complained incessantly about my social life and the late hours I kept.

I finally couldn't take her carping any longer.

I called Mrs. Legg from the office. "I'm not willing to endure your curfew one more night. And since I already have a mother, I certainly don't need or want another one. I'm moving out . . . immediately."

"Good!" she shouted at me. "I don't want some wild swinger living in my home."

Did she even know the definition of a swinger? I wondered.

I gathered up my few possessions, ignored Mrs. Legg as I left the house, and breathed a huge sigh of relief that I'd never have to see the old harridan again.

Heaven translated into a small, furnished, one room with bath efficiency apartment in Spenard. I loved the privacy my little slice of heaven afforded me.

Bill loaned me sheets, a blanket, and towels. At the local Salvation Army store, I collected dishes, silverware, and a few other household items. I couldn't afford to buy a television, but I had a small radio, privacy, and my freedom. Being liberated from Mrs. Legg gave me a new lease on life.

Four

Another new friend in the office, Bee, announced that she was quitting her job in order to return to California. When I asked her who would take over her position, she studied me for a long moment and said, "I can arrange for you to replace me."

I couldn't help expressing my doubt about her chances of success. "I don't have seniority."

"Do you want the job or not?" she asked.

I nodded. "Of course, I do."

Mr. Watson subsequently called me into his office the next day. "You're taking over Bee's position."

I was flabbergasted.

"You'll receive a raise, and a new desk is being ordered for you."

I stared at him, still shocked and quite unable to summon a coherent thought or words of appreciation.

A short while later, I shared my news with April. She reacted to my announcement with tears. "We're a team. I don't want to work with anyone else. How could you do this to me?"

Startled, I didn't know what to say. I assumed that she would adjust to the change, but I was wrong. April didn't work well with my replacement. The two women bickered constantly, never achieving the rapport that April and I had enjoyed.

To add insult to injury, jealousy and resentment reared its ugly head among the other secretaries, who circulated a petition. They felt that Bee's job should have been allotted by seniority, not given to a co-worker who'd been at Alyeska for only two months.

Watson defended my promotion by firmly stating that he'd chosen the most qualified person for the job. Vindication of that sort was sweet, even if it was founded on nothing more substantial that the perception that I was viewed as a superior secretary.

I'd been in the new position for only a few weeks when I noticed a job announcement posted on the bulletin board for Pump Station Number 5. I approached Mr. Watson, asking if I could apply for the position.

He bellowed, "Your raise hasn't even gone through yet, and I've just ordered a new desk for you!" Summoning what little self-control that he still possessed, he continued a bit more calmly, "You'd hate the pipeline, Marilyn. It takes a certain kind of woman to handle working on the pipeline. Trust me when I tell you that you're better off here."

I shook my head, stubbornly restating my request. "I want to apply for the job."

Watson, with notable reluctance, allowed me to complete the application process. Soon thereafter, I received word that I'd been offered the job on the Trans-Alaska Pipeline at Pump Station Number 5. I promptly accepted, excitement gripping me as I anticipated my change of circumstances.

In the end, I was surprised by how much I hated leaving my co-workers, even though I was excited about the prospect of working on the pipeline. I packed my bags, ignored my conflicting emotions, vacated my apartment, and stored my few possessions at Bill Sampson's house.

Although Bill and I had drifted apart in a romantic sense, we'd managed to salvage our initial friendship. He even drove me to the airport for the flight to Pump Station Number 5, wishing me well in such a sincere voice that tears stung my eyes. I concluded that former lovers can be friends after the passion wanes and reality takes over.

"Seize the moment.
Remember all those women on the Titanic
who waved off the dessert cart."
Erma Bombeck

Five

The flight to Pump Station Number 5 landed at the airport at Prospect Creek, which was situated in the flatlands that precede the Brooks Range. As I looked around, I realized that the terrain resembled a moonscape.

I was driven to my lodging, a dormitory single room that reminded me of a narrow shoebox. The absence of a private bathroom assured me that showers would be a community endeavor. Originally, the dormitories had been designed as an all-male affair until a sexual discrimination lawsuit filed by several women forced the powers that be to accommodate female employees with separate dorm rooms and female-only bathrooms.

Cold weather gear—pants, boots, socks, and parkas—was provided by Alyeska. Even the small sizes were huge on my size four frame, since only men's clothing had been stocked by the company's purchasing department.

After unpacking my luggage, I met the Chief Technician, Sam Klinger. Short and rotund, Sam was a chatty fellow who fretted constantly about his responsibilities. He made it his mission in life to run a tight ship at Pump Station Number 5. Little did he realize that he failed miserably, but we all gave him points for sincerity.

My job occupied little of my time each day. I found myself searching for work to do so that I wouldn't expire from boredom. The men employed at the pump station were not accustomed to having a secretary on staff, so I often spent my days reading, fine-tuning my typing skills, or making long distance calls on the Wats Line. This telephone service (Wide Area Telephone Service) was paid by a monthly charge to a company and employees could phone all over the United States as often as they wished. It was similar to an 800 telephone number. I think I contacted everyone I'd ever known within the first few weeks of my arrival at the pump station. In the afternoons, the men shot pool or watched movies.

We could have easily filled the seats at a mini-United Nations gathering. R. & R. (Rest and Relaxation) meant visits with family in Scotland, Hawaii, England, and a variety of other locations across the globe.

Pipeline marriages abounded. While working the line, many of the married men lived with women other than their spouses. Upon flying into Fairbanks, these couples parted company. The men headed home to their legal wives, while the temporary wives amused themselves elsewhere or found new "husbands." Some of the wives—the legal ones—seemed to favor this arrangement, suggesting to their husbands that they extend their employment in Alaska and simply forward their paychecks home.

With more than two hundred men and only a dozen or so women assigned to Pump Station Number 5, the female employees received more attention than any of us really wanted. Invitations were constant, with women viewed as status symbols. Personally, I felt overwhelmed by the glut of available testosterone. I even reached the point of feeling harassed when confronted with unending comments like, "Come to a party with me." "Let's go flying." "How about a movie tonight?" and the time honored "Let's take a drive up the Haul Road."

At night, I'd lock my dorm room door and ignore the constant pounding and verbal entreaties to come out and play. It's easy to feel like a trapped animal in a situation like that. Eventually, I grew accustomed to the attention. I also realized that I might even miss it once I returned to the real world. But while I was on the line, I often ground my teeth in exasperation and prayed for one or two hours of total peace and quiet.

Six

Billy was our janitor. Black, in his mid-70s, thin, and balding, he often slept behind a huge furnace. He tolerated the bigotry inflicted upon him by some of the workers, especially from the Texans in our midst. While he turned a deaf ear to them, I suspect, in hindsight, that his unwillingness to respond to them probably provoked them even more.

Billy saved a seat for me in the mess hall each evening. I often sat with him, enjoying our chats, despite the disdain and resentment expressed by many of my coworkers. Since I hadn't been raised to hate anyone because of the color of his skin, I ignored the jibes and derision directed at me.

I helped Billy with his bank deposits. He could neither read nor write, thus making him dependent upon others. His daughter even wrote to thank me, which really brought home the point of Billy's true vulnerability in a hostile environment.

Although he proposed marriage several times and frequently invited me to his quarters, I laughed off the invitations so as not to hurt his feelings. The fact that I was young enough to be his daughter didn't seem to faze Billy. Ah, sex—the true equalizer! At least, as far as men are concerned!

There was so much money flying around the pipeline, it often seemed as though it was literally falling out of the sky between snowfalls. Waste and theft were rampant. Tales abounded of Alyeska trucks, logos firmly emblazoned on the vehicles, which were spotted as far away as Las Vegas, Nevada and central Florida. A Rolligon, a monstrous piece of machinery that resembles a Caterpillar tractor, even turned up in Arkansas.

Some employees, courtesy of poor payroll accountability, received duplicate paychecks and promptly cashed them. Even when employees died or were dismissed, their paychecks continued. They were always cashed.

A close friend, Mary, knew she was being overpaid. She repeatedly notified the Payroll Department. And they repeatedly ignored her.

Finally, in total exasperation, I advised, "Give it up, Mary. They just don't care."

"But I feel guilty that I'm cheating Alyeska," she protested.

My response might seem a bit odd to most people, but I couldn't help myself. "Don't be ridiculous, Mary. They're cheating themselves." Obviously, there's a definite limit to my patience with corporate stupidity.

As I mentioned earlier, my job left me with way too much free time on my hands. Since I loved flying in the Alyeska helicopter, I obtained permission to ride along to the other pump stations whenever a helicopter landed in our compound.

Greeted like an old friend, I frequently lingered for supper wherever we happened to touch down. We compared mess hall menus in the various line cafeterias. Food on the pipeline was generally quite exceptional. If you were so inclined, you could overindulge twenty-four/seven. Most people, as a result, gained a lot of weight while working the line. The best cooks were employed to keep the employees sated. I have very fond memories of Sunday brunches with seemingly limitless amounts of crab and shrimp piled high on platters.

Several elderly prospectors lived in Wiseman, a tiny village not far from Pump Station Number 5, which was located on the north fork of the Koyokuk River and only sixty miles from the Arctic Circle. Less than fifty residents occupied a collection of log cabins and small houses, the latter built partially underground for insulation purposes. Small trapdoors in the floors of the cabins led to basements where vegetables and other perishables were stored for winter consumption.

Once a thriving community, Wiseman is now a virtual ghost town with a fascinating history. The elderly residents of Wiseman all loved freshly baked pies. We happily indulged them, arriving for our visits loaded down with dozens of pies and an eagerness to hear tales of their years in the north country. In order to satisfy all the residents, we made the rounds each time we visited the village. I savored the stories of the old days as our elderly hosts stroked their long beards and reminisced about the adventures they'd experienced.

Fairbanks, which I visited as often as possible, was a true outlaw town. A friend called me one day to tell me about a dance she'd attended at the Golden Slipper Saloon the previous Saturday night. Apparently, a disgruntled husband had shot his wife while she danced with another man.

Sandy, in a half-amused, half-horrified voice, explained the absurd incident. "Everyone just kept dancing around her body until the paramedics showed up. I got blood all over my shoes. Some people never even missed a beat."

Typical Fairbanks, I concluded, having already experienced some bizarre incidents there. I can't help recalling the tale of the Oregon man who'd worked at Pump Station Number 5. Because they were having marital problems, the man's wife had asked him not to come home for a while. When he finally showed up unannounced, he found a strange man living his life, wearing his clothes, and driving the new car he'd bought for his wife. Talk about disillusioned!

———

When I met Dan Kodiak, a gregarious, compassionate, and very good-looking foreman, I immediately liked him. We often joined a pilot friend stationed at Dietrich, which was located a little more than a hundred miles up the line. Pilot Stan's wife and children lived with him. Their arrangement was a real surprise since families of employees were prohibited from residing anywhere near the pipeline.

No one felt compelled to betray his secret, however, and he often brought along his brood to dine in the mess hall. At that point in time, the pump station was on the verge of closure, as pipeline construction was almost complete.

Dan and I, along with several others, went fishing at No Name River, although Alyeska forbade these excursions. We didn't even need bait! At first we used cheese, assuming that we would need to lure the fish to our hooks. We wound up snacking on the cheese, since the fish were willing to simply leap at our hooks without any form of enticement. The mess hall cooks cleaned and prepared our catch without question.

Dan was a nurturer. He looked out for me, supplying me with my own private cache of wine, fresh coffee, and a white Ford truck with an automatic transmission. Because we were romantically involved, the unwritten pipeline relationship rule kicked in. The other male employees immediately stopped hitting on me, for which they earned my gratitude.

Unfortunately, my boss didn't appreciate my somewhat proprietary attitude about the Ford truck, insisting, "It's not your personal vehicle, Marilyn. It belongs to Alyeska."

I really hated relinquishing the keys, but I sometimes had to. Looking back on my own behavior, I'm surprised Alyeska didn't penalize me.

———

Pump Station Number 5 lacked a television. Radio reception was poor unless you had a powerful antenna. In the evenings, we did enjoy movies, although we didn't have a screen. We made do with a white sheet on the wall.

Despite the absence of TV and other forms of entertainment from the outside world, life at Pump Station Number 5 was tolerable. Bullcooks (well-paid women) cleaned our rooms, provided fresh linens, and the supplies for washing our clothes.

Since our basic cooking and cleaning needs were met, our free time was our own. In truth, that was a mixed blessing. Melancholy thoughts of home, family, and friends invaded the mind like a stealthy plague at times. When one person became afflicted, several more seemed to follow suit. This contagion often yielded groups of depressed people.

To fill my empty hours, I often telephoned people at Alyeska headquarters in an attempt to secure various luxuries. In particular, I persisted until I persuaded those in charge that we deserved an upgraded movie projector and a proper screen for the movies they kept shipping up to us on the supply plane.

As time progressed, I became quite resourceful. Translation: demanding. The result, I'm happy to report, was excellent. True to form, Alyeska invariably responded to my every demand or request with duplicate items. We put everything to good use!

———————

While I was always trying to see what I could get for our pump station, I became friendly by phone with Jean Thomas, who worked in Fairbanks. We talked for hours and I complained to her that we had an old copy machine, which constantly broke down.

Jean said, "Would you like a new one?"

I replied, "Sure. But we won't get one."

"Yes, you will because we have a new shipment coming in and I'll see that you get a brand new one." So, I told everyone at our station about the new copy machine. Their reaction was, "Oh, yeah." I found out later that Jean had a lot of influence because she was sleeping with one of the big bosses in Fairbanks.

A few days later, our new machine arrived and the men were impressed with my influence. However, we didn't have any short paper—just legal size. I called Alyeska and said that we had this new machine but only long paper. Alyeska Supply told me I would have to put in a requisition and wait several weeks for delivery.

Next, I called Xerox and told them my problem. They said, "How much paper would you need?" I told them a few cases would do to just get started. Then they stated they couldn't do this because Alyeska would be upset.

I reluctantly said, "Okay. I will just cut the legal paper to letter size."

Different pump stations were closed because the oil would soon be coming down the line. I told employees who went to these vacant stations that if they saw any letter-size Xerox paper to bring it to me.

One of our subcontractors had asked my boss for copy paper previously and he said he didn't supply subs with paper. Then the paper began to come in.

First, Xerox sent about ten boxes. Hercs (Hercules) are mammoth planes with four propellers and used by Alyeska to carry freight, heavy equipment, trucks, and passengers. There was a rule that when the Herc left Fairbanks, it didn't return for any reason. However, an engineer on the flight told me he was amazed because the plane returned and was loaded with copy paper. People were coming in with copy paper under their arms, and other stations were sending it to us. Sam Klinger, the Chief Tech, was upset.

Dan called me one day and said, "I hate to tell you this, Marilyn, but a big plane just landed and it is full of copy paper." I told him he should be glad I hadn't ordered pencils, but maybe I would do that next.

We had a small trailer filled floor to ceiling with copy paper. Some people thought it was a joke but my boss didn't. He called the subcontractor who wanted the paper before and said, "How much paper do you want?"

She replied, "How much can you spare?"

"As much as you could possibly want."

The men at my station offered to try to use as much as they could. Some copied the Declaration of Independence and others tried to duplicate money. Everyone was trying to use the paper so I wouldn't get into trouble.

Whenever someone called me from the pipeline saying, "We understand you need paper," I would reassure them that we didn't. My boss refused to discuss copy paper at all.

In fact, after I left my job and several years later, I bumped into an engineer in an Anchorage store who said, "Remember all that copy paper in the trailer? We are still using it and there is plenty left." I thought I would never hear the end of the copy paper fiasco.

Dan was laid off and returned to Oregon. He called me a few times and wanted me to quit and come down there, but I didn't want to give up my job for an uncertain future. I never heard from him again, although I missed him for a long time.

———·———

Bears wandered in and around the pump station all of the time. They were a routine sight. Employees were told not to feed or otherwise encourage them, but some ignored the directive, even though it was very dangerous to do so.

I soon learned that our bears craved donuts, and they stole them at every opportunity. The bears evidenced a genuine dislike for Sam Klinger, charging at him whenever they saw him. Sadly, the feeling was mutual.

The bears received points for cleverness. They frequently broke into the kitchen to gorge themselves on cans of fruit cocktail, but they never touched the other canned goods like carrots or peas. The bears were quite willing and able to destroy a truck or a car if they scented sweets, salt and grease-laden potato chips, or meat hidden within it.

———

When I met security guard Kenny Richmond, I immediately liked his sense of humor. His Southern drawl was pure Alabama, and when he spoke I felt waves of warmth wash over me. Kenny was an artist. Whenever he left a note for me, he always added a sketch of Omar Mung.

We spent a lot of time together despite the fact that he was married.

Working on the pipeline resembled living on another planet. Hence, a whole new set of societal rules seemed to apply to all of us. Once our co-workers realized we were a "couple," we were on everyone's list of people to be invited to any activity, official or otherwise.

Following a week long trip to Fairbanks for truck repairs, I discovered Kenny's tender nature. The night of my return to the pump station, I found a drawing of a strange looking little man on my pillow, a tear slipping from one eye and a printed message that read, "Guess who misses whom?"

Thus began the Omar Mung drawings. I never learned the reason for the little man's name, but Kenny did finally share his origins. Sometime earlier, before Kenny left Alabama, a friend of his had gotten drunk and claimed he'd seen an odd looking little man. Also drunk, Kenny had urged his friend to describe the little man's appearance in detail. Kenny then drew the image of the man, including a tall hat and shoes that turned up at the toes and contained tinkling bells.

Omar Mung assumed a life of his own. He turned up every-where. I'd open my mailbox and find a drawing of Omar. He appeared on the wall in my room, in my clothes closet, and then in the main dining room. Wherever I went, Omar Mung put in an appearance. I even found Omar etched into the ice on the windshield of my truck.

Kenny's romantic inclinations steadily grew. I introduced him to Rod McKuen's poetry, and he subsequently wrote a letter to me with lines from LISTEN TO THE WARM included in the text. Sadly, I no longer have all of those letters, notes, and sketches. I truly regret not saving them.

Seven

In 1977, the Teamsters Union held a great deal of power in Alaska. One of the Teamster foremen time-carded me when I drove a dorm-mate to the airport. That was the day on which I realized just how protective the union was about their control over jobs on the pipeline.

In the midst of layoffs at Pump Station Number 5, a young Teamster driver showed up for work. Several Senators and Congressmen obtained employment on the pipeline for their sons. The paycheck was excellent, the demand for the positions acute. The young driver, Bob Holloway, was a clean-cut college kid, who'd received the job because his father was an important man in the hierarchy of the Teamster's organization. The men at our station openly resented him, and they made every effort to turn his life into a living hell whenever possible.

I befriended Bob, initially because I felt sorry that he'd been ostracized through no fault of his own. I came to genuinely like him as we became better acquainted. Most of the time, no one even spoke to him or allowed him to sit at their table in the cafeteria. The Texas oil workers possessed a notably harsh attitude about Bob.

When I asked Bob why he stayed on the pipeline, his reply

helped to remind me of his youthful vulnerability when he said, "I don't want to disappoint my father." His words continued to ring in my ears long after he finally gave up the battle and departed Pump Station Number 5.

Bob Holloway managed, though, to cause a final ripple of controversy on the day of his departure. The Teamster hierarchy arranged for him to take the seat of another pipeline worker already confirmed on the flight. The resentment borne of that action resonated for a very long time. I privately applauded the event, viewing it as minor payback for all of the abuse and insults he'd endured during his time at Pump Station Number 5.

When Bob stopped by my dorm room to say goodbye, I wished him well and resumed my life. A few weeks later, a Teamster Business Agent approached me in the cafeteria of the pump station.

"I need to speak privately with you," he said.

I agreed to meet with him, more out of curiosity than anything else. After all, I wasn't a Teamster.

Kenny objected to the whole idea of a private meeting with the Teamster Business Agent. He also voiced cautionary words about the reputation of the Teamsters, which was at an all time low following the disappearance and probable murder of Jimmy Hoffa. I calmed Kenny by agreeing to call him once the meeting ended.

As it turned out, the Teamster Business Agent wanted my testimony about Bob Holloway's treatment at the pump station. He began our conversation with the remark, "Mr. Holloway would like to express his appreciation for your kindness to his son."

Baffled, I said, "There's no need. Bob was a nice kid, and I felt sorry about the treatment he received."

"Still, Mr. Holloway heard through the grapevine that you'd like to drive for the Teamsters. We're more than willing to send you to truck driving school. At no cost to you, of course."

Chapter 7

I thought enviously of the $50 per hour that the Teamster women I knew earned on the pipeline. Because I was only making $7 an hour at the time, this was very tempting, but I felt reluctant to become obligated to people with such questionable reputations. I had jokingly told several people that I wanted to be a truck driver because they were making big money. The Teamsters heard this and that is why they gave me the offer.

When he noticed my hesitation, he continued, "We can arrange another job for you, whatever and wherever you'd like. In exchange, we'd like you to come to Fairbanks and testify about the treatment Bob Holloway received at Pump Station Number 5."

I imagined then the fallout and the reprisals that might occur. "I'm not interested, but thank you for your offer."

He persisted. "We'd make it worth your while if you testified."

I refused and I considered myself very fortunate that I was never again approached by anyone representing the Teamsters. Much later, courtesy of the hindsight that plagues us all, I came to the conclusion that I'd been a fool not to jump on the Teamster gravy train.

Eight

The work on the Trans-Alaska Pipeline was winding down. I was excited to have been a small part of the building of the pipeline. As our time at the pump station drew to a close, we celebrated our collective success with a plaque that contained the names of those who'd worked at Pump Station Number 5. The men also created other mementoes, including Alaska maps made from the pipe with an image of Omar drawn on one of them by Kenny Richmond. I still own these treasures.

The oil flowed down the line initially on June 20, 1977. No one slept that night as we awaited the big event. Rumors flew that reporters like Connie Chung and other high profile newscasters from the Lower Forty-Eight would be present to report the first big gush of crude oil through the pipeline. Some people even predicted that the pipeline would fail and that the oil would never make it to its destination. The latter group was wrong, of course.

Like an implacable ribbon of silver, the completed pipeline traversed eight hundred miles of Alaska terrain from Pump Station Number 1 at Prudhoe Bay on the Arctic Ocean to the oil control station at Valdez. A much-heralded engineering feat, the pipeline carries millions and millions of barrels of crude across three mountain ranges and assorted earthquake fault lines for eventual transfer to the waiting oil tankers. I still have the message page that came over the teletype machine at the Pump Station on June 20, 1977 as oil coursed through the pipeline for the very first time. It reads, "Please tell the waiting world that we have oil in."

Deafening cheers sounded as the real celebration commenced. It lasted for weeks. Pump Station Number 5 employees also received an invitation to one party in particular hosted by Alyeska. Our initial enthusiasm was dampened when we realized that most of us wouldn't be able to attend the festivities because we had to work.

I telephoned Public Relations at Alyeska, pointing out that their gratuitous invitation contained a back handed slap in the face since we all had to work. When I threw in the word "discriminatory," a reference to the pump station work crews who'd received the invitation, Alyeska's senior management saw the wisdom of dispatching air transport to collect all of the employees at the various pump stations. The result was that a volunteer skeleton crew remained at each pump station, while the majority of the employees were free to attend the weekend party at the Castle Hotel.

Speeches, dinner, dancing, and flowing rivers of booze ensued once we arrived via the private jets. I'd had enough partying by Sunday afternoon of that memorable weekend, and I willingly boarded the flight back to the pump station. I was surprised when I realized that I was the only passenger aboard the aircraft.

Sam Klinger waited for me at the airport. He immediately demanded, "Where is everyone?"

I shrugged as nonchalantly as possible. "I guess they all missed the flight."

Sam, angrier than I'd ever seen him, ordered the pilot to retrieve the others. "Tell them that anyone who's not aboard the next flight will be fired."

Once I had some privacy, I hurriedly telephoned the hotel and left messages for as many people as possible. The plane was full when it returned to the pump station.

For the sake of historical accuracy, I would be remiss if I didn't note the development and utilization of a revolutionary pipeline inspection device known as the Superpig. The 5,000 pound, 14 foot long Superpig, which operates in a flowing stream of oil as it moves at a normal rate through the pipeline, was designed to map both the interior and exterior of the 800 mile long Trans-Alaska Pipeline.

Powered by a rechargeable, self-contained battery pack, the Superpig provides an early warning detection system of any change, shift, or curvature in the pipeline, as well as measuring and recording both the temperature and pressure within the pipeline. From an ecological perspective, the benefits are obvious.

Once the oil came in and the pipeline was officially up and running, I traveled to Canada for a visit with my family. I returned to Alaska, driving the car I'd stored rather than via an airline. I also rendezvoused with Kenny. We both knew our relationship would soon end. As a result, our time together was a bittersweet experience for both of us. Kenny would soon return to his wife, and I was about to open a new chapter of my life in Alaska.

"When one door of happiness closes, another opens;
but often we look so long at the closed door
that we do not see the one which has been opened for us."

Helen Keller

Nine

Anchorage yielded a few boring secretarial jobs in 1978, first at the Union Oil Company and then at Arco, and an unpredictable social life that included a Seattle millionaire, who tabulated each and every expense on the calculator he wore suspended from a cord around his neck like a piece of ostentatious jewelry. I decided then and there that millionaires weren't worth the aggravation.

I came to the same conclusion about most of the men I encountered at work and in social situations, basically because they were such a collection of oddballs and misfits. Alaska women have a saying about the men there: "the odds are good, but the goods are odd."

It didn't take me long to realize that I missed the pipeline and the people with whom I'd worked. And I missed Kenny Richmond, even though I understood the necessity of consigning him to memory after a memorable farewell interlude he arranged before his wife arrived in Anchorage to set up housekeeping with him.

While working at Arco in 1980 for a group of environmental engineers, I learned of a secretarial position at the Naval Arctic Research Lab (NARL) in Barrow, the northernmost point in North America aside from the North Pole.

You can't imagine Barrow until you see it firsthand. It's the largest Bush community in Alaska with a population of about three thousand souls. Barrow is less than twelve hundred miles from the North Pole. Called "the Top of the World," Barrow occupies flat, open terrain—miles and miles of nothing but tundra.

Summer in Barrow translates into twenty-four hours of light each day since the sun doesn't set between May and August. High temperatures reach thirty-five to forty degrees on a good day. Conversely, the winter months are frigid and snow-filled, with temperatures plummeting to minus one hundred degrees with the wind chill, and are composed of seemingly endless stretches of darkness. During the winter whiteouts and blizzards that pummel the area, it isn't at all unusual to see huge, lumbering polar bears wandering about the community in search of food and shelter.

Barrow's population is a motley mix of Inupiat Eskimos, Filipinos, and a modest number of Tanniks (white people) from a variety of cultures across the globe. When I resided in Barrow, the antipathy for all Tanniks was apparent. During one election, a mayoral candidate's campaign was actually founded on a platform designed to rid the area of all Tanniks. However, this failed.

Yet another experience in dormitory living awaited me when I arrived at the naval station. Executives assigned to NARL routinely occupied furnished homes, drove vehicles supplied by the Navy, and pumped free gas whenever needed. While everyone else in Barrow conserved the gasoline they purchased, the executives often left their cars and trucks running for hours at a time in order to keep the motors warm.

The inequities of the situation didn't escape me or anyone else not authorized to receive similar privileges. Executive wives even got into the act by securing jobs in Barrow, earning $20 per hour despite the fact that most of them didn't possess a single secretarial skill. One executive wife called me on her first day of work for the Barrow Police Department asking for instructions on how to turn on an electric typewriter.

How I envied those women their fat paychecks, their easy access to Watts lines for calls to the Lower Forty-Eight, and the convenience of simply stopping by the naval station grocery store (similar to a military commissary) to pick up whatever they needed at no charge. Many of the men employed at NARL were university level instructors on loan to the naval station. They often commented that they'd never had it so good. I couldn't help but agree.

Although provided with my own dorm room, I shared a bathroom with several other floor occupants and took my meals in a cafeteria with a surprisingly eclectic menu. The chief cook would often prepare special treats for the residents he liked. In my case, he discovered my passion for cream puffs and satisfied my craving.

Like life at any small outpost, intrigue, gossip, and one-up-manship prevailed even among the senior ranking officers and executive level civilian employees. Each department operated like a mini-fiefdom, and there was little or no cooperation between departments. The conflict and bickering quickly wore thin, and I made it a practice not to become entangled in the petty machinations whenever possible.

An unexpected bright spot appeared on the Barrow horizon in the person of Reiko, a Japanese woman hired as an accountant. A lively, intelligent, and good-humored woman, Reiko had graduated summa cum laude from Puget Sound University in Washington with a degree in accounting.

Although considered a management level employee, she was assigned quarters in a dormitory. The rationale utilized by the university and NARL was that she wasn't married and didn't require a house for personal use. Discrimination rearing its ugly head! Reiko, who always selected her battles with care, decided not to make waves about her housing dilemma. She made the best of a truly stupid situation.

Despite the cultural and professional gulfs between us, Reiko and I became great friends. We turned a deaf ear to our supervisors when they pointed out that Reiko was management and I was a lowly secretary. The implication that fraternization was inappropriate annoyed us both, since our friendship harmed no one.

Always alert for ways to earn extra income, Reiko and I stumbled upon an opportunity to teach at the Inupiat University of the North. (NARL, eventually closed as a cost-cutting measure by the Navy, became the site of the Arctic Sivunmun Ilisagvik College.) We received $25 an hour for teaching, whether or not the enrolled students showed up for class. Reiko "frunked"—she couldn't say flunked to save her life—many students when they failed to attend her classes.

I did the same in the speedwriting class I taught.

Reiko's friendship sustained me that winter when my former husband, father-in-law, a favorite aunt, and my 16-year-old nephew all died within a few months of each other. When you combine these personal losses with the sense of isolation prevalent during the winter months in Alaska, you can well imagine the battle I waged against being swamped by the depression I felt.

While rumors swirled that NARL would soon be closed, Reiko and I devised a plan to remain in Barrow. There existed the potential in Barrow of employment with good wages. Reiko managed our job hunting, her negotiating skills superior to my own. Interviews ensued, one in particular with a Native corporation appearing to be the most promising. After Reiko negotiated our salaries, benefits, housing, furnishings, and transportation while I looked on in shocked amazement, the personnel manager accepted our terms and extended offers of employment.

We promptly gave notice at NARL, assuming that our plan wouldn't backfire. We couldn't have been more wrong. While NARL accepted Reiko's resignation, my boss attempted to persuade me to remain until the naval station actually closed. I was offered everything from a new office to an assistant to a salary increase. Admittedly, I was tempted, but I resisted.

Gossip initiated by my boss's wife and one of her friends, an employee at the Native corporation, resulted in the accusation that I was simply angling for more money and that I had no intention of actually leaving NARL. In short, I was supposedly attempting to manipulate my current employer, which couldn't have been farther from the truth.

The personnel manager of the Native corporation, upon learning of the situation, rescinded his offer of employment to me. Reiko's offer remained intact since her departure from NARL caused no conflict. The personnel manager explained that his company was dependent upon NARL for contracts. I understood his situation, but I certainly didn't like it.

I, of course, was in the miserable position of having given notice on one job and having my new job offer withdrawn. I remained at NARL in Barrow, due in large part to my own stubbornness and Reiko's pledge that she would assist me in finding a good job when the time was right.

Ten

Still determined to find new employment in Barrow, I continued to explore my options while I worked at NARL. I wasn't the only person searching for a job in those days, and I knew that I needed to be alert to every possible opportunity no matter where I was or what I was doing. One evening, while out dancing with friends at PowMain, the early warning site located approximately ten miles outside of Barrow, I introduced myself to an attractive man seated alone at a table.

Lonnie Richards was a superintendent at a major Barrow construction company. As we danced and chatted, it occurred to me that I should ask him to help me if I applied for a position at the company where he worked.

I began dating Lonnie soon after, unaware that our relationship began with the lie that he was divorced and had a son. It wasn't until much later, during my recovery from major surgery in Anchorage, that I learned the truth from Reiko about his marital status and that he was, indeed, married and had four children. Suffice to say, our relationship unfolded like a roller coaster on a damaged track, and, like most damaged things, it ultimately failed, but not for several years.

After too many mishaps to itemize, both personal and professional, I accepted a temporary secretarial position with Sohio Oil Company at Pump Station Number 1 at Prudhoe Bay. Located on the Arctic Ocean and the Beaufort Sea, the pump station was situated in a wilderness of taiga (translation: land of little sticks) and tundra, part of the 80,000 miles of the North Slope Region of Alaska. Best described as a frozen desert, permafrost in the region ran to a depth of three thousand feet.

Abundant wildlife populates the area, and it isn't uncommon to see moose, Dall sheep, caribou, grizzlies, musk ox, wolves, and a wide variety of birds.

I plunged into my work at Prudhoe Bay with a vengeance. Despite the lack of any real work, I was still determined to demonstrate that I was worthy of becoming a permanent hire rather than a temporary employee. The pump station at Prudhoe Bay was wonderfully modern and filled with conveniences from a first class dining facility, a movie theater, to a jogging track for the exercise-minded.

Not long after arriving at Prudhoe Bay, Lonnie contacted me with the news that my father had died. I was devastated, because I'd assumed that, although he was ill, my father would rally once again and I would be able to see him the next time I could afford a holiday. I immediately flew home to Canada, and I remained there for two weeks.

During my absence, Lonnie took a message concerning a job at Sohio from their personnel office, but he failed to give it to me. Only later did I learn that I'd been offered a permanent position, but Lonnie had turned it down on my behalf without telling me. Despite the fact that he claimed to be proud of the fact that I was working on the pipeline, he secretly resented the distance between us.

Although I did return to Prudhoe Bay for another temporary position, my goal of a permanent job on the pipeline was never realized. Reiko saved the day when she called me from Barrow to tell me about a teaching job that was being advertised in the local newspaper. I might have had a degree in English, but I'd never really been a teacher, except for my brief stint as an instructor at the night school in Barrow.

I telephoned the Alaska Business College. My employment interview was conducted during that phone call. To my utter amazement, the school hired me, leaving me in a state of panic about my ability to actually teach in a traditional school environment.

———

The sense of community among the teachers at the business college in 1981 was an unexpected blessing. Drawn into the fold upon my arrival, I received friendship and guidance from the other teachers on staff at the Alaska Business College. I definitely needed their expertise when I realized that I'd been hired to do the impossible, which was to teach typing, the use of magcards (Magcards were before computers. This machine could save documents onto magnetic cards. Each card held a couple of thousand characters of typing. Cards were then entered into a machine where you saved the documents and made your revisions later), spelling, English, legal and medical transcription, and shorthand all in one class.

Fortunately, most of the students were patient with me. They seemed to realize the difficulty of teaching so many subjects simultaneously to twenty or more students. I did my best, though.

My students were an eclectic lot. This was as much a consequence of state funded study programs that placed unqualified individuals in my classroom as people desperate to escape their various personal problems and bury themselves in their studies.

Alaska Business College was my proving ground. By that, I mean that I proved to myself that I could handle just about anything in an academic environment! As it turned out, those lessons in flexibility and patience stood me in good stead as the future unfolded.

———

At Anchorage Community College (ACC) in 1982, I taught in the Office Skills Program and also took Teacher Education classes. I took to ACC like a duck to water. I loved teaching, my students were frequently women eager to gain expertise that would offer them post-divorce economic stability, and my fellow teachers were all women. An all female teaching staff could have been a nightmare, replete with catfights and inter-departmental bickering. Instead, it was a sisterhood of intelligent women who supported, encouraged, and assisted one another.

While teaching at ACC, I decided that obtaining my teaching credential would provide me with both financial stability and the prospect of some kind of a retirement fund. I was nearing my fiftieth birthday and, like many people, I'd lived in the moment for most of my adult life.

The added complication was that in our on-again, off-again love affair, Lonnie still hadn't divorced his wife and was adamantly opposed to my studies. He even refused to shoulder a more substantial portion of our household expenses or to assist me with tuition, so I gritted my teeth and took out a student loan.

Although it was difficult to admit, I knew in my heart that I couldn't count on anyone but myself. I didn't see Lonnie's passive-aggressive behavior for what it was at the time, but the combination of his criticism about my poor financial planning and his refusal to be supportive of my efforts to obtain my teaching credential proved to be yet another nail in the coffin of our dysfunctional relationship.

Hindsight now offers me an even better perspective on our relationship, in that, like many women of my generation, being with the wrong partner seemed (at least, at the time) better than being alone. And then, of course, we have the time-honored maxim that love can, and often does, make one exceedingly stupid!

Eleven

I became a homeowner for the first time in Alaska as a result of a special, low-income housing, subsidy program. The subdivision was still under construction when I discovered it in an area just south of Anchorage. Thanks to a talented realtor, who guided me through document completion and meetings with the bank officer and the escrow company, and a short-term $1,000 loan from Lonnie, my dream of home ownership was transformed into reality.

I moved into the house during the Christmas holiday season, ready to enjoy an unrestricted view of the mountains from my kitchen and an equally beautiful view of the woods from the living room. Once I rescued my stored furnishings and unpacked, a real home began to take form. I couldn't have been happier.

Lonnie occupied the house with me, and we agreed to share expenses in a 50-50 split. Otherwise, I couldn't have managed the house payment on my own, although I confess to being angry when I discovered that Lonnie made ten times my annual salary when he worked construction.

And I further admit to being furious when he charged me to build a single car garage next to my modest, two-bedroom house. If I owned the house now, I'd still be waiting for Lonnie to install the insulation in that garage. Another major building project, the fireplace, nearly resulted in a homicide. I'll let you guess who'd still be standing!

Once I moved into the new neighborhood and became acquainted with my neighbors, I discovered that all of the homeowners on my street were women. We were beneficiaries of a new Low Income Housing Assistance Plan in Alaska. I pitied any man foolish enough to move into our neighborhood. The poor guy would have been mobbed.

The U.S. Postal Service didn't deliver to the subdivision for one very simple reason—we didn't have individual or community mailboxes. Our builder had neglected to install them, and none of the women seemed inclined to attempt to accomplish this feat. The ground, especially in the middle of the winter, was frozen, so digging a hole and sinking a post in cement implied a major challenge.

Melissa O'Rourke, the attorney who lived across the street, embraced the challenge. Much to the collective shock of both her neighbors and the men wandering in and out of our neighborhood one frigid Saturday, Melissa actually succeeded in erecting a viable post in a deep hole with a mailbox affixed to it. The post and the mailbox still stand today. I consider the entire affair a testament to female grit and determination.

Twelve

During the next few years I settled into multiple roles—teacher, student, and homeowner, to name a few. I also traveled periodically, visiting Hawaii and several California locations whenever the winter months became too oppressive. Sometimes Lonnie joined me, but most of the time he didn't.

Our relationship continued to episodically deteriorate and then revive, as though operating independently of us. The trips I took alone offered brief respites from the arguments and the stress of dealing with his wife and children, but the bottom line was simple. I was involved with a married man who was allergic to anything but the most superficial kind of commitment. In truth, I was nearing the end of my ability to rationalize Lonnie's behavior, even though I'd been raised to always search out the positive aspects of other people's personalities, especially those I loved.

Following one of several California trips and my return to Alaska, I finally completed the last of my University of Alaska classes and made the decision to obtain my Master's Degree in Reading. I took the advice of several teachers, ignoring Lonnie's predictably negative reaction to my pursuit of an advanced degree, and registered for an accelerated summer school program at the University of Southern Mississippi. I was determined to become a full-fledged, certified teacher, despite being almost fifty and lacking any real traditional teaching experience.

I spent the next summer at USM, along with several other Alaskan students, taking a full load of classes in order to maximize my time there. I enjoyed the campus, the other students, and the local community of Hattiesburg. The people of Hattiesburg accepted the students of USM. The more mature of us often went dancing at the local watering holes on the weekends.

My mentor at USM, Dr. Fleming, took me under her wing, offering me general academic guidance when I needed it and the use of her personal library whenever I wrote my class papers. I occasionally dated some of the men I met in the local community, attended a wide variety of off-campus social gatherings, and, on lazy Sunday afternoons when studying became impossible in the oppressive heat, I toured antebellum estates that graced the area.

When several of the Alaska Master's Degree students approached the dean and requested early exams to facilitate our departure for home at summer's end so that we could prepare for our student teaching, the dean and the professors all agreed to accommodate us. I deviated from the plan, however. Having been told that I could attend a required class to complete my studies at the University of Hawaii, I decided to fly there and combine studying with an R&R before returning to Alaska.

I departed the University of Southern Mississippi with excellent grades for all of the classes I'd taken. I felt a great deal of pride, especially because I'd struggled with the math class required for student teaching. My math professor had faxed the syllabus and my course grade to the University of Alaska. The results were "accepted," thus allowing me to qualify to join the ranks of the latest crop of student teachers once I returned home.

Bad news awaited me at the University of Hawaii. The class I'd planned to take had been cancelled, but I hadn't been notified prior to my arrival in Honolulu.

With only a credit card in my wallet and almost no cash, I couldn't persuade anyone other than the Holiday Inn to accept my credit card.

A recent spate of stolen credit card usage had soured most retail establishments and restaurants on accepting anything but cash from out of town visitors. Finally, a local bank advanced me the funds I requested and charged the amount to my credit card. I paid off my lodging and room service charges and made a beeline to the airport.

More than anything else, I wanted to get home to Alaska. When I stepped off the plane at Anchorage International Airport, I felt like kissing the ground like the pope does when he arrives at his destination.

———

Student teacher positions were at a premium in Anchorage, and I was unsuccessful in my pursuit of one. Because I'd spent a lot of time working in Barrow and had maintained my friendship with Reiko, I contacted her, explained my dilemma, and asked her for advice. She immediately went to work, canvassing the local schools and chatting with the various principals on my behalf.

On the personal side of the equation, returning to Alaska hadn't solved any of the relationship issues with Lonnie. I announced my plan to accept a student teaching position in Barrow at the North Slope Borough School District, and his reaction was predictable. He moaned, groaned, and just generally made life so miserable for me that I couldn't wait to pack my bags and head north. One particular conversation shortly before my departure for Barrow still sticks in my mind, because I wound up championing Lonnie's wife.

To make an exceedingly long conversation much shorter, suffice to say that Lonnie refused to incur the financial losses of a divorce. He categorically declined to accept the rational reasoning that his wife deserved half of their assets if they divorced. When I reminded him that she was a stay at home mom and the primary parent for their four children, he went through the roof. From his perspective, he'd earned the money and so it all belonged to him. I found his position stupid and said so, which didn't earn me any points at all.

Lonnie accused me of abandoning him for student teaching in Barrow. He also said he wouldn't support the endeavor in any way. Since he'd never supported my educational pursuits, his threat sounded hollow and I ignored it. When he stormed out of my little house, I felt a wave of total relief wash over me.

After arranging for a friend to keep an eye on the house during my time in Barrow, I prepared for the trip. My funds were limited, because I'd spent nearly all of my savings on graduate school, but I purchased the groceries and warm clothing essential for my stay there. I carefully packed my trunks, bought an airline ticket to Barrow, and resigned myself to being on the tightest possible budget during my student teaching.

When I arrived in Barrow in 1982, the trunk with the food supplies was missing. A fellow passenger on the flight, an officer with the Barrow Police Department, took pity on me and volunteered to drive me to Reiko's apartment. The officer and I dated casually for a while, but a definite absence of chemistry eventually ended the relationship.

I resided very briefly with Reiko and her son in their one bedroom apartment until I found a room for rent with Carrie and

Tom Billings, a school district employee and a maintenance worker. I did my student teaching at the Ipalook Elementary School under the guidance of Marcella Kingsley, a gracious and popular twenty-eight year old teacher. With thirty students to corral in the classroom each day, we had our work cut out for us.

Barrow schools provided much more than academic instruction to the students. A large percentage of the children routinely appeared for class without proper clothing. The teachers distributed jackets, mittens, and hats to students in obvious need. Additionally, we dispensed vitamins, breakfasts, lunches, and snacks, and we supplied the implements for proper oral hygiene. We all realized that without these perks, many of the children would go hungry or suffer frostbite in the frigid winter temperatures.

Despite the overt animosity expressed by the Barrow Native population to all Tanniks (white people), most of us ignored the shouted insults and rude gestures directed our way. It wasn't difficult to understand the anger of the Natives. They'd endured the devastation inflicted on their people and their culture courtesy of the influx of white developers and various other private and governmental groups for several generations. Whenever Reiko was mistakenly identified as a member of the Native population, she received reprimands because she didn't speak the Inupiat language. She generally ignored the rage aimed at her.

Teaching, I felt certain after less than a month in the classroom, was my mission in life. I loved every opportunity to teach the students, and I dreamed constantly of having my own classroom.

I enjoyed doing the class bulletin boards, and Marcella appreciated my eagerness to do the task since she felt little enthusiasm for it.

Money, always a problem, became a huge issue during my stay in Barrow. Desperate, I called Lonnie and asked him for a modest loan until I could find a part-time job to sustain myself. The lecture that followed simply validated his disdain for my dream of becoming a teacher and his general lack of respect for me as a woman. When Reiko realized my predicament, she once again exhibited her innate kindness and friendship. She handed me an envelope, which contained $150. I used the funds to pay my rent and purchase food, the latter a necessity since the trunk of food-stuffs I'd shipped with Alaska Airlines still hadn't shown up.

The trunk eventually arrived, but the contents had spoiled. I wrote a letter to Alaska Airlines, explaining what had happened. Subsequently, I received a phone call from the airlines. We all knew they bore no responsibility to reimburse me for spoiled perishables, but God was watching out for me it seemed. I received a $200 check from the airlines a short time later, and that generosity of spirit on the part of Alaska Airlines further persuaded me that I was meant to be a teacher.

The principal of the school learned of the financial strain I was dealing with and offered me part-time employment supervising study halls and the gymnasium used by the students in the early morning hours. The weather made outdoor recess virtually impossible in Barrow, and the students were permitted to play games in the gym before classes commenced each day. Today, Ipalook School has an entire indoor playground for their young charges with slides, swings, and other paraphernalia suitable for recess.

As well, I found part-time employment inputting data for the Director of Special Education so that written records could be shredded. A catastrophe occurred when the custodian, misunderstanding a written directive from me which said, "Take these to the dump" took all of the shredded records and the highly prized shredder to the dump for disposal. I never got over the feeling that the Special Education Director blamed me for the loss of that paper-shredding machine, especially since he personally went to the dump and searched for it, but to no avail. The custodian, clearly a very literal sort of fellow, said he was simply following my instructions.

I found additional part-time employment as an instructor of speedwriting at the Inupiat University of the North, and substituted for various elementary teachers if they fell ill or had other obligations. With the increase in my income and a student loan for tuition, I also enrolled in two graduate level classes for my degree in Reading.

Although I experienced bouts of loneliness for my life and home in Anchorage, I still nursed mixed emotions about the situation with Lonnie. Ever hopeful that he would somehow undergo a personality transplant and become a more supportive person, the time we spent apart served to mute my awareness of his flaws as a man. I also continued to socialize, trying to take my mind off Lonnie, but, in truth, I still missed him. Old habits die hard, don't they?

———

I fell in love with one of my students, a delightful little second grade boy with shining dark eyes and straight black hair. From a fatherless home, Payuk was bright and enthusiastic. His mother sold drugs, and she was on the verge of being incarcerated. Payuk, despite his youth, was responsible for rousing himself and his two little sisters each morning for school. Sadly, he was often absent from school, largely because of any substantive parental supervision.

When Payuk told me that he had several fathers, I realized the true instability of his home life. Even more disturbing was his desire to change his name from Klvantisc to Rogers, simply because the latter name was easier to spell. I assumed that the name Rogers actually belonged to one of the parade of men his mother bedded when she wasn't in trouble with the law.

Payuk had an irrepressible imagination. He made up tall tales that were vastly entertaining but also symbolic, I thought, of the instability of his home life. His vivid imagination took him on trips to Washington, D.C. to visit the president and winging off into the night sky to rescue me when he thought I was in jeopardy.

Barrow students.

He preferred to sit with me during the lunch hour at school, as opposed to joining his classmates. More evidence, I sensed, of his longing for a strong mother figure. I adored this child, but also realized that his troubled home life was clearly damaging his view of the world and his self-esteem.

Even my host teacher, Marcella Kingsley, whose judgment I normally respected, voiced her concern over the amount of attention I lavished upon Payuk. Although I tried to step back and be more objective about the boy, I regretted the necessity of such behavior when I saw how dejected he looked. The sadness in those normally shining dark eyes sent a stab of pure pain into my heart.

A mishap with hair color application had me appearing in school one day with shockingly white hair. Students and faculty alike peppered me with questions until Payuk, deciding I'd endured enough verbal harassment, ordered everyone to cease and desist. Then, with the innocence that is the province of only the young, he plopped down beside me and held my hand. Had the need arisen for him to slay dragons on my behalf, I'm confident he would have met the challenge with enthusiasm and determination.

When Payuk arrived at school one morning covered with bruises and abrasions, I quelled my horror at his condition, silently damned his mother, and asked him what had happened to him. He insisted that he'd fallen down while playing. I obviously didn't believe him, since children in Barrow rarely, if ever, played outdoors in the dark Alaska winters.

Several teachers privately voiced the opinion that Payuk's mother would probably allow me to adopt him if I made the offer. I gave the idea a great deal of consideration, because I was so fond of him.

Realistically, though, I felt too old, nearing fifty, to start raising a seven-year-old child. I also worried that relocating him to Anchorage would result in a level of homesickness that would cause him to attempt to return to the only home he'd ever known. With the wisdom inherent in hindsight, I now regret that decision. I could have provided him with a modest but stable lifestyle, encouraged him to attend college, and given him the love and nurturing he so richly deserved. Today, Payuk isn't simply a high school drop out, he's also homeless and a substance abuser.

As my student teaching days came to a close in Barrow, I received evaluations from Marcella Kingsley, the teacher with whom I worked, the principal of our school, and then from the head of the Department of Education. The final evaluation proved to be the most rigorous and nerve-wracking.

Marcella absented herself from the classroom for three days so that my teaching style and skills, as well as my ability to interact with all of my students, could be observed and scored. Even though I was terrified at the prospect of being judged inadequate, I received a good evaluation and the University of Alaska was subsequently notified that I had satisfied the requirements of student teaching.

I would have liked to remain in Barrow as a full-time teacher. Salaries were high, in the $60,000 annual range, depending upon experience and educational credentials. Housing, however, was at a premium. Although the Special Education Department asked me to stay on and accept a position as a full-time substitute teacher until a permanent position was available, I couldn't find a place to live and, as a consequence, I had to decline their offer.

With Carrie and Tom already preparing to depart Barrow, I would soon be on the street. Talking to the superintendent of schools proved useless. Housing was provided for contracted, full-time teachers, but not for substitutes. Since he made no effort to assist me in obtaining housing, I concluded that returning to Anchorage was my best option.

I packed and flew home to Anchorage. Lonnie met me at the airport and drove me home, where I discovered that my friend

Kathi-Jo had taken excellent care of my little house during her stint as a house-sitter. I was delighted to walk into my home and find the stereo playing, warm lights glowing, a vase of fresh flowers on the kitchen counter, and a box of chocolates waiting for me as a welcome home gesture from Kathi-Jo.

Thirteen

Securing a permanent teaching position proved to be a major life challenge and a lengthy test of my endurance. I began the process by substitute teaching in several of the Anchorage area schools. To say that it was a harrowing experience would be an understatement.

Students considered substitute teachers fair game for every insult and accusation under the sun. They seemed to sense on some primitive level the true vulnerability of substitute teachers, and they took great delight in creating as much mayhem in their lives as possible. As a consequence, substitutes learned to fear their students. Any accusation of cursing at or hitting a student contained the potential of sabotaging a substitute's teaching certificate, thus eliminating that individual's ability to ever be hired as a permanent teacher and also causing the substitute to be reported to the Teachers Standards and Practices Committee.

Equally challenging was the no-holds-barred attitude among certified teachers in search of the few permanent teaching positions that were available. Fierce competition ensued, and some very bizarre tactics emerged among the competitors. Nothing was sacred. From catered meals, to out and out sexual seduction of those in charge of the hiring process, and every deplorable tactic in between, the entire process reminded me of a squadron of buzzards circling a carcass, each nasty buzzard jockeying for the optimum flight path to the carcass.

I did manage to do a limited amount of substitute teaching in the Anchorage School District, as well as teaching secretarial skills at the Anchorage Community College and word processing at the Computer Institute. I also sought and received part-time work as a tutor for the school district and with several private students. The road was a long one, but I slowly advanced along its path and gained the teaching experience I needed.

———

After a great deal of prayer, endless part-time jobs, and substitute teaching experiences, a turning point occurred in my quest for a permanent teaching position. In 1985, I desperately contacted the Alaska Teacher Placement Service office in Fairbanks. Dedicated to the placement of teachers in permanent teaching positions throughout Alaska, the service had an available slot for a Reading and English instructor at a high school in Napaskiak, a tiny Bush village.

Although my certification was for elementary level teaching, my area of expertise was Reading and English. I pressed the point, repeatedly reminding the Teacher Placement Service representative of my specialization. I also emphasized the fact that I could easily teach high school age students thanks to my experience as a community college teacher.

In October of 1985, I received a call from the high school principal at Napaskiak, who asked for references regarding my teaching ability and my rapport with the students under my supervision. Rave reviews from Patricia Swanson at the Alaska Business College resulted in an offer of immediate employment.

Since Lonnie was still in my life, I didn't look forward to telling him that I would be departing soon for Napaskiak. I sensed that accepting the teaching position would yield absolutely no support from him and would end our relationship once and for all. I was right, although, like a beached fish still gasping for life-sustaining oxygen, our love affair made a few attempts to survive as I made the transition and settled into my life in Napaskiak. Too busy with the preparations necessary for an imminent departure, I did not mourn the potential demise of our relationship.

Complications also arose as I tendered my resignation at my various part-time jobs, but, in the end, nearly every one of my employers graciously accepted my desire to teach in the Bush and accustomed themselves to my decision. I hurriedly packed clothing and teaching supplies, ordered food items for shipment, rented my little house to a military couple, and set out for what I hoped would be a satisfying new life in Napaskiak.

First stop: the Eskimo city of Bethel, just forty miles from the Bering Sea and situated at the mouth of the Kuskokwim River. A transportation, supply, and medical hub for surrounding villages, Bethel's modest airport served two major airlines.

The school district's personnel director met me when I arrived in Bethel. After I signed all the necessary documents and was informed that some of my luggage and supplies would have to be brought to me later, I boarded a small private plane for the final six-mile leg of my journey to Napaskiak. I soon learned that there were no roads into or out of the village. As it was, the small plane used an empty field adjacent to the town for incoming and outgoing passengers.

Napaskiak was little more than three square miles of dilapidated wooden dwellings. It was also home to Yupik Eskimos, Natives who spoke the Yupik language and who were primarily dependent upon fishing for their subsistence in the harsh northern regions. No one waited to meet me when I stepped off the small private aircraft, but the kindness of a stranger, who escorted me to the local school and introduced me to the principal and his wife, proved to be my salvation.

A cordial greeting by the principal and his wife and a less than appetizing lunch preceded my first view of my new residence. I was stunned by the rundown condition of the place, which included broken window panes, a few decrepit pieces of furniture, animal droppings everywhere, filth encrusted appliances, a floor that I was certain had never been cleaned, and no plumbing or running water. I promptly sat down and wept over the disaster zone I was expected to call home.

Three teenaged boys, who had been dispatched by the principal to assist me in tidying up the shack, arrived a short while later. They found me in a state of shock as I wandered from room to room in the ramshackle hovel. Their arrival calmed me somewhat. They hauled buckets of water from a nearby well, and we all began the cleaning process.

As I scrubbed, I reminded myself that I needed practical teaching experience and, despite the miserable living conditions, I would have to tolerate the situation in order to achieve my goal. Bear in mind, though, that frozen blades of grass protruded through the slats of the wooden floors, the wind produced a constant whistling sound as it penetrated the roof line and walls, and my toilet facility was what is commonly known as a "honey bucket."

For the uninitiated, a "honey bucket" is a pail lined with a plastic bag and often topped with a toilet seat by the clever soul inclined to improvise when seeking basic creature comforts. Believe me what I tell you that I had fantasies about flush toilets for several months!

———

During the years (1985-1988) in which I lived in Napaskiak, I grew to genuinely appreciate the village and the people who resided there. Even though I was a Gussak (white person), the villagers accepted me.

With a core population of about two hundred and fifty individuals, it was a humble Bush community with wood frame houses in varying states of disrepair, the yards filled with abandoned appliances and machinery and other piles of unidentifiable debris. But, Napaskiak also boasted a general store, a post office that relocated with alarming regularity, courtesy of the quixotic moods of the postmistress, the school in which I taught, and a federally funded Headstart facility.

The absence of a hospital in the village always troubled me, especially given the unsanitary water situation and the resulting intestinal maladies, virulent cases of influenza, emergency situations, and a variety of other medical conditions for which most people routinely receive proper medical care. I tried to be very careful, especially with the tainted local water. A few drops of bleach in the water container I kept in the kitchen provided me with a certain amount of peace of mind. The water in Napaskiak had over the recommended levels of arsenic, which stays in your body.

The nearest medical facility, which was in Bethel, could only be reached by air or by dogsled along the Kuskokwim River, the latter a veritable freeway for snowmobiles, taxis, trucks, sleds, dogsleds and pedestrian traffic when the river was frozen solid. Having traveled by dogsled to Bethel when flying wasn't feasible because of adverse weather conditions during the winter months, I can attest to the risk of additional injury inherent in that particular mode of transportation if one had suffered a serious back injury or unset broken bones.

My Napaskiak home.

As I settled into life in Napaskiak, I discovered the fondness of the locals for steam bathing. Nearly every back yard contained an adapted structure of some sort—even a boat—that allowed the users to "steam" in relative comfort. Dry spruce or alder wood was used to fuel the stoves, and buckets of water poured atop the heated rocks generated the necessary "steam" for the steam baths.

Steam bathing had both practical and social implications for the villagers. Groups of men often congregated to "steam" and chat; the village women chose to "steam" separately in order to gossip; and young people found the privacy they desired in the steam baths, the resulting pregnancies regarded with neither distaste nor disapproval among the good natured villagers. Legitimacy seemed a non-issue for any child born in the village. Instead, each newborn was welcomed with love and acceptance.

Although a general store existed in Napaskiak, it was a disappointment. The scarcity of fresh fruits and vegetables made me imagine the sensory pleasure of a simple tossed salad or a fresh apple. Even when those items appeared at the store, they were already brown with rot. I called the end result a "tundra" salad. Whenever I traveled to Anchorage, I always made a point of stopping in at a restaurant that had a salad bar in order to satisfy my constant craving for fresh fruits and vegetables.

The school in Napaskiak combined both elementary and high school classes. A dozen teachers, seven women and five men, oversaw the academic, music, and physical education classes conducted there. I must admit that most of the male teachers weren't people worthy of admiration or emulation by the students.

In fact, many of these men were, for the most part, a selfish lot who seemed to resent the possibility of academic success by their students; some even sabotaged potential success by certain students and then attempted to bully me into cooperating with them. My refusal to penalize Special Education students with lower grades for poor academic performance resulted in more than a few verbal brawls, but the principal supported my teaching style and trusted my judgment about these students.

Like any small group of people, the teachers represented both the positive and negative elements of human nature. As a result, some of them truly cared about and displayed a genuine devotion to all of their students.

Other teachers, however, possessed an obvious I'm-getting-by-while-I-collect-a great-paycheck mentality that made me want to scream with outrage. At the very least, this latter group was guilty of neglecting the educational needs of the young people they were employed to teach, and of failing to motivate them, both personally and scholastically, in constructive ways.

The teachers, as a group, also evidenced all of the personality dysfunctions, inadequacies, and biases typical of any collection of human beings gathered in one place to perform a specific task. Several rose to the challenges inherent in teaching in the Bush, but, sadly, some did not.

———

Discipline, I quickly discovered, was accomplished easily with my Reading and English students. Their very healthy addiction to basketball, not to mention their desire to play the game, prompted them to do their homework, participate in class, turn in class assignments in a timely manner, and just generally help out when asked to clean blackboards, run errands, or empty the trash cans.

Basketball practice games after normal school hours required an adult in attendance in the gym. I volunteered to act as their sponsor, despite being urged by other teachers not to permit the kids to intrude upon my off duty hours. How could I deny them the opportunity to stay out of trouble? The answer, as far as I was concerned, was simple. I couldn't.

Many of the boys who played basketball openly voiced their conviction that the NBA would want them once they graduated from high school. I didn't take it upon myself to correct this belief. I knew that dealing with the real world and all of its disappointments would happen soon enough.

My Napaskiak students proved to be like night and day when compared to the hostile Anchorage students I'd endured as a substitute teacher. I was grateful for their core decency and the respectful manner in which they treated me. Oh, of course they teased me and joked with me, but their pranks were mostly harmless bids for attention.

Senior class students frequently expressed their desire to obtain good jobs in either the private sector or in the military upon graduation from high school. Since English was a second language for a majority of the students, I endeavored to stress the value of improving their language ability.

I realized that many of the graduating seniors would be tested during the pre-employment interviewing phase of the hiring process. The results of the California Test of Basic Skills given to the students were a sobering reality check for them. They suddenly grasped that they all had a great deal of work to do if they were to receive passing grades on the test as they sought employment in the world beyond the tiny village of Napaskiak.

We also worked on composing résumés and letters of application, as well as term papers, short stories, personal journal writing, and poetry.

As a matter of routine I read aloud to my students. Louis L'Amour's *The Last of the Breed* fascinated them, because it told the tale of Sioux Cheyenne Air Force Major Joe Makatozi (Joe Mack), who was captured by the Russians in Siberia during the Cold War era. He escaped his Soviet pursuers, surviving the unforgiving climate and harsh terrain of the Siberian landscape courtesy of his wits and Native skills.

Inferiority complexes plagued many of the Native students, and those feelings were reinforced by the fact that everyone in authority in their world was white. In order to level the playing field in the white world for them, I conducted mock scenarios during which the students ordered food in a restaurant, used the telephone, and interviewed for jobs.

Napaskiak party.

Although I saw no need to produce Ms. Manners' clones, I also taught them the etiquette required when dining out at the home of a friend or in a restaurant. And I introduced them to Shakespeare, one of my personal passions. The result, which was praise from both the students and their parents, validated and inspired me as a teacher.

All was not ideal in Napaskiak, however. As in any community populated by flawed human beings, there were undercurrents of violence and aberrant behavior that couldn't be ignored. Incest and child molestation were not uncommon, nor was sexual abuse and the battery of spouses. The dominant causes, at least from my perspective, were alcoholism, unemployment, and extreme poverty.

Some of the teachers, and I include myself in that number, remained watchful for signs of physical and sexual abuse among our students.

But even though we made the appropriate reports to the authorities, the families and victims often denied the accusations. As a consequence, little or nothing was ever done to safeguard many of the children in true jeopardy.

As we all know from our own life experiences, hopelessness is yet another malady that can occur among human beings for one reason or another. Napaskiak was not exempt from this sad condition of the human spirit. There were tragic incidents of suicide among the students in the community. Fortunately, those types of deaths did not happen too often. That they happened at all still saddened me greatly.

The conflict that existed between the time-honored "old" ways and the "new" ways that existed in the world beyond the borders of the village was quite apparent among the students. Their parents and the elders of the village urged them to remain in the community after graduation and embrace the traditional ethics of life and living. In sharp contrast, teachers encouraged them to learn new skills in order to obtain employment in the cities or to further their educations by attending college.

Adding to this conflict was the ingrained cultural belief that one is obligated to honor the wisdom of the village elders by acquiescing to their counsel. A combination of respect for the elders and feelings of intimidation as a result of my students seeking new and different ways of embracing the future could, and often did, produce disastrous results. I frequently witnessed this cultural tug of war first hand, and I can attest to the anxiety, and subsequent paralysis of purpose, that it frequently generated in my students.

As often as was practical, I urged my students to find inventive ways in which to integrate the old ways with the demands of contemporary mainstream life in Alaska. I felt strongly that maintaining respect for their cultural background, while also making every effort to adapt to the expectations and norms of the larger world into which they sought entry and future success, would serve them well. Although many of my students made a sincere attempt, only a handful achieved success.

————————

Prom nights are always a big event in the village. From the catalog, the girls ordered long gowns, some with hoops, and boys purchased suits and tuxedos. They wanted me to have a date for the prom.

There was an old man whom they told me was half-blind and walked with a limp and he would be great for me. I agreed that we might be a match if he were really half-blind. Every time he would go by the window with his dog team, they would point to him and say, "There he goes, Mrs. Forrester. He would be fine for you. He has a wood stove so you would have heat, even if the generator went out. And you might even get to drive his dog team." An additional benefit was that he had traps and I might acquire a fur coat.

They couldn't understand why I wasn't interested. They hated to see anyone by themselves and were constantly trying to match me with Larry Leap, a parsimonious teacher I did not like. When I was teaching, some of the students would hop with their fingers over their desks to tease me about Larry Leap.

Kenai, a bright-eyed Yupik girl, asked me if I had a husband. I said he was dead. "Do you have any kids?" I replied that I didn't. They she queried, "Do you have a mother and father?" I told her they were dead also.

She said, "Oh, you poor thing. We will find you someone."

Working on the prom, I was fortunate to enlist the aid of an artistic student, Jimmy Nicholas. He did the decorating and stayed late into the night hanging silver and gold streamers and flowers. We purchased a rose arbor and the graduates entered through it. The king and queen sat on a throne at the end of the gym, while a silver revolving globe spun in the center of the room. The girls in their evening dresses danced with partners to out-of-date taped music played on a stereo.

Napaskiak prom.

It was different from a big city prom but it was a wonderful night for them. A pre-prom dinner was served to all villagers, and I had to buy the food. Students served the guests, and the regular school cook was hired to prepare the food. They had saved the money to choose whatever they wished to eat. I was ingratiating to the cook because the year before he became angry, and one of the teachers had to cook. I did not want that to happen to me.

The seniors chose crab, shrimp, and strawberry shortcake. Then they requested china plates and silverware, not plastic. I wanted our graduation to be special for them, so I flew into Bethel to borrow dishes and silverware from the school district. When I came back with all these boxes, everything needed washing. After the meal, I helped clean up, and we had to rewash all these dishes. It was a nightmare! Then I had to take the dishes back to Bethel by plane. Later, I got a terrible migraine and missed a day of school.

However, the students maintained it was, "The best graduation prom and dinner ever."

"You have to count on living every single day in a way you believe will make you feel good about yourself—so that if it were over tomorrow, you'd be content with yourself."

Jane Seymour

Fourteen

I found many rewarding opportunities for personal self-improvement during my time in Napaskiak. Among those opportunities was instruction by local village women sufficiently skilled to guide me through the complex process of creating a mink-trimmed pair of calfskin boots, a beaver hat, and beaver mittens lined with rabbit fur.

While we sewed, the ladies gossiped and, in broken English, shared with me the news of the village. They seemed to take great pride in the fact that I was the only white teacher who sewed with them. I was baffled by the reluctance of many of my colleagues to become better acquainted with the mothers of their students and the Native culture that had such a profound impact on the children we taught each day.

Friendship, with local villagers, despite my Gussek status, was borne more out of my desire to be a good teacher and a participant in the community than in any deliberately planned agenda on my part. I think the sewing ladies, the aides who worked at the school, and the other women teachers viewed me as just one of the gang.

We gossiped, planned celebrations, commiserated with one

another when a relationship failed, and just generally behaved as any group of women in an isolated community would. I suspect that the very nature of the isolation of our remote locale was the glue that held us together in times of stress or when personality differences created a rift among members of any of these loosely constructed groups.

——·——

Although I was promised an improved dwelling by the principal upon my arrival in the village, I didn't really expect him or the school district to fulfill that promise. I moaned and groaned for months, of course, and when the principal grew tired of my complaining, he advised me to stop griping and be happy that I was warm, dry, and saving money.

I'll concede that he might have been right, but I still loathed the dilapidated shack in which I lived. Teachers and other village residents were able to shower once a week in the gym at school, and we laundered our soiled clothing on a strictly enforced schedule. Communal "steaming" just wasn't on my priority list of things to do, especially since it would have been a group experience.

I forgot about the promise of new living quarters after a while, and I'd long since stopped complaining. What would have been the point?

Then, out of the blue, a barge transporting a three bedroom, two-bath mobile home appeared on the Kuskokwim River. The entire village turned out to mark the event. Even the students dashed out of their respective classrooms in order to witness the arrival of my new home.

The bathroom and kitchen facilities and the washer and dryer, thanks to an absence of running water in the village, were a moot point, of course. However, the sheer size and cleanliness of the mobile home persuaded me that I must have died and gone to heaven.

The lengthy delay to reside in my new home, because the Bethel school district authorities seemed in no hurry to hook up my electricity, only slightly dampened my enthusiasm. I harassed the school district until they set the situation right with the local power company.

When I finally moved into my new home, which was situated less than fifty feet from school property and in the same neighborhood as the homes of the other teachers, I felt as though I'd moved from a cardboard box shelter in a Watts alley to a mansion in the Hollywood Hills. Friends and strangers alike turned up to inspect the mobile home. At one point, I grew so exasperated with all the curious lookeeloos that I considered charging a fee for tours of the trailer.

Another aspect of my life in the village entailed my involvement with students during non-school hours. I routinely organized overnight slumber parties at school for the girls after we'd all gone sledding. I escorted my students on a variety of outings, including field trips out of the village in order to increase their familiarity with the landscape and peoples of other communities.

I also conducted Friday night Bingo games, candy the prize for the winners. After all, I didn't want to encourage the emergence of an entire generation of village gamblers!

During my tenure as a Special Education teacher, I made every effort to give a party at least once a month for my students, during which we played games, watched video taped movies, and engaged in sports activities, primarily basketball. Their need to develop socialization skills was acute, and I refused to ignore that need simply because a few people frowned over use of my off-duty time.

Special Education students came in all sizes, shapes, and temperaments. Often the victims of fetal alcohol syndrome, these kids tested every last nerve I owned, but I still loved them. A few students had a propensity for explosive violence that seemed rooted in the frustration of poor communication skills and by the clear understanding that the average students and several of the teachers at our school looked down upon them.

Their hunger for attention and acknowledgement prompted me to employ more patience than any so-called "normal" student could ever reasonably expect from me. I must confess, though, that being punched by a Special Education male student or suddenly becoming the unwitting target of a projectile pitched across the room wasn't much fun. Behavior modification techniques, which I learned during a summer spent in Oregon while I obtained a Special Education teaching credential, helped somewhat, of course.

One of the other things I attempted to do at the school was to level the playing field for my Special Education students. By that, I mean that I made a concerted effort to persuade my fellow teachers of the wisdom of grading the Special Education students based on their commitment to learning, class attendance, and the overall effort to learn that they expended, rather than grading them as they would an average student.

My efforts earned me a great deal of resistance—less, I was happy to note, from the female teachers than from the men. Of course, I was subjected to the very vocal ire expressed by several of the teachers. They were absolutely convinced that the changes I was proposing would render meaningless the grades earned by their regular students.

A few of the teachers even suggested that the distinction of "special education student" should be noted on the graduation certificates. However, Alaska state law prohibited this kind of prejudicial distinction.

It was with great relief that I found support for my endeavors from the State Coordinator for Special Education, who subsequently paid a visit to our Bush school. She made a presentation to the teaching staff in order to expand their grasp of the unique needs of Special Education students. She also reminded them that all of the school districts operated under the supervision of the State of Alaska. Thus, the Coordinator and her staff were empowered to enforce the Special Education laws and policies in all of the school districts, and, as far as she was concerned, there would be no exceptions!

Not all my colleagues were persuaded by, or happy about, her cautionary remarks, of course. On the heels of the Special Education student controversy, I was blackballed for several months by some of the less understanding male teachers.

However, I still derive enormous personal satisfaction in having made an effort to rectify a system that seemed intent on the destruction of the self-esteem of these special needs children—the same system that prevented them from participating in extracurricular activities like sports because their grades were so poor and which left them feeling like third class citizens.

Fifteen

From a personal point of view, Christmas in an Alaska Bush village could be a really depressing experience. The locals were, in large part, members of the Russian Orthodox Church. It was their practice to celebrate Christmas in mid-January.

We nonetheless made an effort to enjoy a festive Christmas holiday season and celebrate the birth of Jesus in a way and at a time suited to our own traditions. Still, it was usually a muted and somewhat lonely affair. The one really bright spot that occurred during the holidays involved roving groups of carolers, who were rewarded for their melodic efforts with handfuls of candies that we tossed from our windows.

———

Without ever intending to, I found myself in the position of taking on the role of the unofficial counselor to village women experiencing everything from marital disharmony because of alcoholism, to spousal and child abuse, to behavioral problems with their children. All this in spite of the fact that my first marriage had ended in divorce and I had never had any children of my own.

In my own defense, I believe that these women grasped the depth of my empathy and compassion for the issues they faced as wives and mothers. With the benefit of hindsight and maturity, I think that all one needs to do is to listen when a troubled person feels compelled to confide a personal concern or to simply vent their accumulated frustrations. The result is that, with sufficient kindness and encouragement, they often determine their own course of action to resolve problems.

———

The Native population of Alaska receives monetary compensation, both federally and state-mandated and funded, to assist them in obtaining food and shelter. In many communities, the local Native residents are also recipients of housing that is constructed on their behalf by the State of Alaska.

The dilapidated condition of several existing village houses, which were occupied exclusively by the Native population, prompted a request by local authorities for the building of additional homes. Twelve, lovely, new houses were built as a consequence of this request. I must admit that I would have been happy to claim any one of these homes as my own personal residence.

Rental fees for these new houses were evaluated on a case-by-case basis and determined solely by the annual income of the prospective Native tenant. The downside of these state-built homes quickly became apparent, however. The absence of both running water and a sewage system in the village rendered useless the bathrooms, laundry rooms, and kitchen sinks of these well-intentioned dwellings.

Chapter 15

Funding from both the state and federal governments also benefited the teachers who taught school in the Bush village. A seemingly endless budget, strictly supervised by the school principal, was made available for use by the teaching staff. As a result, we received authorization to order all of the books, educational games, bookshelves, miscellaneous classroom furnishings, and nearly any other supply that we deemed necessary for teaching.

The Industrial Arts instructor took particular pleasure in expanding his cache of tools, nails, and various other mechanized equipment suitable for use by his shop students, courtesy of the generous funding allocated for our school. His students were never without proper supplies, and his classes enjoyed understandable popularity.

Additionally, the excess budgeted monies available for use by the principal of our school, allowed him to procure an extensive fur supply for use by villagers who wished to sew fur items for personal use and sale. The end result was the creation and subsequent production of numerous fur-lined hats, pairs of boots, and mittens. A local villager was employed by the school district to instruct students who wanted to learn the traditional skills, which would allow them to create these practical necessities of survival during the winter months.

To some people, this latter expenditure might seem a superfluous and inappropriate use of educational funds, but the significance of it didn't escape the educators committed to students who faced cultural discrimination at every turn. Fostering a new skill and encouraging pride in one's heritage often results in a viable means of teaching self-respect and raising an individual's self-esteem.

Sixteen

I felt genuinely enriched on a personal level and viewed myself as a competent teacher as a result of the time I'd spent with my students in Napaskiak. When I was offered a teaching position in the community of Palmer, I considered the situation with great care and decided that I wanted to accept this new opportunity.

First, though, I realized that I would have to discuss the situation with the Lower Kuskokwim School District. Since I'd signed a contract with the school district, I knew that I couldn't pretend it didn't exist and simply walk away. I would need their cooperation and permission in order to nullify my commitment to them.

I telephoned the Personnel Manager for the school district, explaining that I'd received, and was inclined to accept an unexpected offer of employment in the city of Palmer. The manager immediately put me on notice that the district would initiate a complaint against me with the Alaska Teacher Standards and Practices Commission.

Basically, he warned me that my teaching credential would be revoked, I would be fired from my current teaching position, and a formal reprimand would be placed in my permanent file. As if that triple threat wasn't weighty enough, he then announced that

I would also be subjected to the indignity of being sued by the school district for breach of contract.

Stunned by his angry pronouncement, I barely managed to whisper a weak, "Thank you for explaining the situation to me." Then, I shakily re-cradled the telephone receiver. It was a very long time before I felt my respiration return to normal.

When the phone rang a little while later, the caller was a good friend. She proceeded to inform me that the Personnel Manager for the school district had notified the principal and his wife of my recent telephone inquiry.

Obviously, I wasn't willing to abandon all of the sacrifice and struggle I'd endured to become a teacher. Nor was I eager to be robbed of my teaching credential, regardless of any desire on my part to accept the proffered teaching position in Palmer, which was situated on the roadway system and not tucked away in an isolated village community.

I telephoned the Personnel Manager a second time, informing him that I had declined the Palmer School District's offer of employment. I also told him that I had every intention of returning to teach at the school at Napaskiak. When he went on to caution me not to penalize my students for the school district's stance and my thwarted attempt to dissolve my contract, I took great exception to his comments.

I assured him with all of the dignity that I could muster at that point in a nerve-jangling day that I was far too professional to ever penalize a student for the vagaries of the adult world or the school district. And so I returned in August to teach during the fall term at the village school.

—·—

The night the furnace in my small mobile home blew up was

one of the worst experiences of my life. At the time, frigid sub-zero temperatures dominated the region, with minus one hundred degree readings being recorded by the weather bureau courtesy of the wind chill factor.

Despite my initial plea for help to the construction workers employed to make repairs at the school and the existence of several unused generators, I failed to persuade these men to come to my rescue. I spent that first night, and several subsequent nights, sleeping wrapped in a blanket on the floor at the school. The only saving grace of the situation was that my mobile home was located next door to the school, so it was a relatively short hike to find a semi-warm retreat from the winter elements.

What I discovered when I returned to my modest home in order to retrieve some clothes sobered me considerably. A case of sodas stored beneath my bed had exploded and quickly frozen.

The entire kitchen floor had also been transformed into a skating rink, thanks to the exploded bottles of vinegar and other liquid items stored on my kitchen shelves. When I stepped into the kitchen, I slid across the ice-covered floor and slammed into a small table, also frozen in place. Without that table as a barrier, I would have kept on sliding and crashed through the kitchen window.

I can laugh now when I recall the situation, but, at the time, I was reduced to tears of utter frustration and self-pity.

"Parts for the generator might take weeks, perhaps months, to arrive," cautioned the maintenance man who took care of the school district dwellings rented to the teachers.

So, I approached the construction workers again, proposing that they loan me one of their spare generators so that it would be warm enough for me to return to my little trailer. When they countered with the offer that I could rent one of their extra generators for a daily fee, with the proviso that I would also pay for the gas to power the generator, I eagerly accepted their terms. I would have gone into debt for the rest of my life in order to be warm and sleep in my own bed.

———•———

Annual floods were considered to be a matter of routine by the villagers. I didn't consider them at all routine! In fact, I was terrified when the Kuskokwim River overflowed its banks and began flooding the entire village at an alarming pace.

As I emerged early one evening from the home of friends after dining with them, I came to a dead stop when I spotted the swiftly rising current of water that appeared to be on the verge of consuming the village. I was fortunate that two young students saw me and volunteered to escort me to my home. I quickly accepted their offer.

When we reached my home, I hurriedly gathered items that I feared would be lost if the floodwaters entered my mobile home, and put them up on a high cupboard for safekeeping. As the water continued to rise, I was advised to climb atop my roof if I felt threatened.

The villagers all seemed to take the rising waters in stride, using small rowboats, various other inflatable forms of transportation, and large slabs of Styrofoam to make their way about the village. I watched them with no small amount of shock at their casual acceptance of what I considered to be an impending catastrophe.

I stayed close to my radio, listening to the flood watch bulletins. I learned a great deal that day about spring ice melts as I simultaneously monitored the situation by radio, watched the recently built town boardwalk float away, and prayed for deliverance.

The flood tide turned back just as suddenly as it had arrived. To my utter amazement, I observed the waters steadily recede, leaving huge pools of muddy water, all manner of debris, and the expanses of sucking mud that we would all have to navigate on foot in the days and weeks ahead.

———·—

Lonnie popped up on my personal radarscope shortly after the spring flood. He'd always been a force of nature in my life, so his sudden reappearance didn't really shock me. He'd already visited me a few times during my stay in the village, usually with little or no advance warning.

We hadn't resolved anything about our relationship during his forays to the Bush. I couldn't help wondering why he bothered to show up at all since our relationship had completely run out of gas by then.

I was still single. He was still married. What more is there to say when it's obvious that a man has no intention of changing his marital status?

I had already decided that we were finished, and all that remained for me to do was to persuade him of that indisputable reality. Predictably, he wasn't at all receptive to my message that our love affair was officially over.

Lonnie went to great effort to persuade me that I should continue to indulge him and his need of me. When I resisted, he made all of his usual empty promises. In the final analysis, he failed. I'd learned my lesson. Lonnie was, in that regard, an excellent teacher.

———·—

After four years in the village, I had satisfied my contract with the school district and was free to seek a teaching post in a new locale. Although I'd attempted to secure a position in nearby Bethel, it was clear to me that district politics, of which I was woefully ill-equipped to be a viable participant, and teacher favoritism would work against me.

I traveled to the Alaska Teachers Job Fair in Anchorage during the month of April. Résumé and teaching credentials in hand, I very optimistically applied for a permanent teaching position with the Anchorage School District. Then all I could do was to wait and to pray for a positive response.

At the end of the school year, I said farewell to my students in a letter. I revealed my plans to depart the village of Napaskiak, reminded them that they'd been my very first students, which made them extremely special to me, and I promised them that I would always remember them with deep affection.

Happily, I am still in touch with a few of my very first students. My hope is that they remember me with the same affection that I feel each and every time I think of them.

Seventeen

Alas, my fantasy of teaching and living in the thriving community of Anchorage was destined to remain a fantasy. I spent the entire summer in a state of sheer frustration. The few interviews I'd managed to obtain were a dismal failure, probably because of the anxiety I experienced every time I faced a prospective employer.

The lesson I learned that fateful summer: maturity doesn't necessarily ease one's fear of rejection.

At my wits end one day, I began telephoning the various school districts, hoping that a teacher had declined a position at the last minute and had left one of the districts in a staffing bind. The Matanuska-Susitna Borough School District superintendent offered me no hope of placement on the faculty of a school in his district. However, he did share with me the news that he'd had a recent phone call from the school district in Kotzebue. The district was desperate to replace a Special Education teacher who had unexpectedly decided to withdraw from the position she'd accepted at the Kotzebue middle school.

I contacted the Northwest Arctic Borough School District that same day. Their Personnel Manager invited me to interview for the Special Education teacher vacancy. He sweetened the invitation with the offer of an all expenses paid, round trip. Of course, I immediately accepted his invitation.

———

Kotzebue, 1989-1991

The town of Kotzebue is located on a three mile long spit of land known as the Baldwin Peninsula where the Kobuk, Noatak, and Sezawick Rivers meet. Five hundred and forty-nine miles from Anchorage and twenty-six miles above the Arctic Circle, Kotzebue had about three thousand residents. It was also the second largest community above the Arctic Circle.

The winters in Kotzebue are eternally dark, and summers rarely exceed mid-50s temperatures with thirty-seven straight days of daylight. But on the night of August 8th each year, one has the opportunity to witness two separate and distinct sunsets. Hard to imagine, but it's true.

Kotzebue is the hub of the region for air travel arrivals and departures, as well as all manner of commerce, culture, and outdoor activities. Also, there were three schools, a hospital, and the Maniilaq Health Center for local residents.

The primary mode of winter transportation in Kotzebue was by snowmobile or dogsled. It's interesting to note that approximately twenty-six miles of roadway exists to accommodate the use of trucks, personal cars, and motorcycles during the few months each year that these can be utilized by the local population.

Entry into Kotzebue was achieved solely via aircraft or barge traffic. There weren't any roads into or out of Kotzebue from other population centers.

I was interviewed by the school district's Personnel Manager upon my arrival in Kotzebue. An offer of employment was immediately tendered for my consideration. I accepted the school district's offer to teach at the Kotzebue Middle School without a moment of hesitation.

The Personnel Manager counseled me to initiate my search for suitable living accommodations as soon as possible. Unlike Napaskiak, housing designated specifically for rental by the teaching staff didn't exist in Kotzebue.

Immediately, I began my quest for housing, but I quickly learned that I faced yet another challenge—extremely limited options with regard to the rental of an apartment or a small home. In many cases, families in Kotzebue doubled up in one dwelling, or groups of singles shared a medium sized dwelling.

The local technical school offered to temporarily house me until I found a place to live, which gave me a limited amount of peace of mind. By the time I was ready to return to Anchorage to get organized for the move to Kotzebue, I hadn't made much headway in my search for living accommodations. Although I'd located a geodesic-style rental house that I liked, I'd been cautioned by the owner, a teacher, that a prospective tenant had already reserved the dwelling. I asked her to contact me if the arrangement fell through, but I wasn't very hopeful.

Somewhat disheartened by my lack of success, I made my way to the local airport and prepared to board my flight back to Anchorage. As I waited, I received an unexpected phone call from the teacher who owned the geodesic house. She informed me that the tenant she'd expected to occupy the house had cancelled. She then offered to rent the house to me. I promptly accepted, promising to forward a deposit for fuel and the first month's rent check to her as soon as my flight landed in Anchorage.

Thrilled that I would soon be teaching again, even though I wouldn't be in Anchorage, I packed my belongings, rented my house, and arranged for my return flight to Kotzebue.

I had a job and a place to live. Reasons to celebrate!

My Kotzebue home.

A new style of teaching—known as "inclusion"—awaited me when I arrived at the middle school that first day. I knew that not all teachers appreciated this style of group teaching, i.e. the regular classroom teacher, a gifted student teacher, and a third teacher. That third teacher would be me. I was more than willing to give the "inclusion" style of teaching a fair try.

A shortage of teachers at the Middle School in Kotzebue also necessitated my assignment by the principal to teach two additional classes, Mathematics and English. I worried about taking on these additional responsibilities, because Special Education teachers already have the task of producing a lot of extra documentation about the progress being made by their students, along with supplementary testing of those students. These tasks, which help to guarantee the funding of the Special Education classes in any Alaska school, are mandated by both the school district and the state.

Predictably, chaos ensued in the form of neglected Special Education students and the total lack of discipline in the classrooms. I hold the principal of the Middle School culpable for both problems. Traditional school discipline was unnecessary, she'd insist whenever the subject of out of control students arose. She then advised her teachers to devise "loving" methods in order to control the behavior of their students.

I did not agree. Common sense dictates that all children in a school setting need clearly defined academic expectations, a structured environment in which to learn, and the disciplinary rules that reflect acceptable behavior within our society as a whole.

I longed to change schools and teach in a saner and more civilized academic environment, but even that pursuit seemed doomed, and brought down upon my head the wrath of the school district. I even considered admitting defeat and returning to Anchorage, but I decided to bite the proverbial bullet and remain in Kotzebue for purely economic reasons.

Like most people, I needed to work for a living, but employment hustling drinks in some third rate bar in Anchorage wasn't exactly how I envisioned spending my future. Neither was clerking in a grocery store, for that matter. I had a specialized education, and I was determined to use it in order to make my way in the world.

So, I persevered, teaching those few adolescent-aged students who actually came to school to learn and coping with those inclined to all manner of disruptive behavior.

I managed to make a few friends along the way that first year, a fact for which I am still very grateful. Their kindness and compassion frequently steadied me when I reached the boundaries of my tolerance.

———

A formal Teacher Evaluation, which is one of the tools used to determine if a teacher will be retained for the upcoming school year, by the school principal can be a daunting and fear-inspiring experience. The principal of our school spent several hours seated in the rear of my classroom, seemingly oblivious to my rattled nerves and furiously wrote comments on her note pad. I held my breath and prayed the entire time.

Some of the male students in my classroom were determined to misbehave that day. I'm delighted to report that they saw the wisdom of walking a straight and narrow path when I quietly threatened to have them permanently suspended from all basketball games.

Life lesson: You achieve control in the classroom in any way you can manage the task!

When I finally found the courage to open my Teacher Evaluation envelope, I was stunned by the results. The principal's praise left me confused. My good friend and fellow teacher, Wanda, observed that the principal wouldn't dare to give me a negative Teacher Evaluation. She'd piled too much work on me to risk portraying me as anything but a splendid teacher.

While living and teaching in Kotzebue, I worked as a Reading tutor after school. I also spent several evenings each week helping out in the library. At long last, I was financially stable, which was no small accomplishment given my erratic financial status during the previous ten years.

My modest geodesic-styled house evolved into a long-standing test of my flexibility. From furniture arrangement—there wasn't a square or rectangular shaped room to be found in my unusual home—to the time-honored frozen water pipes—pretty typical in Alaska homes. I still managed to cope. Although there were times when I wanted to give in to the panic I periodically experienced.

Imagine if you can, being trapped in your house at the height of the winter season when the temperatures plummet and the only door to the outside world is frozen solidly to the door frame. Now, I know exactly what you're thinking—use the phone, dummy. Great idea, but I couldn't call out for assistance, because the phone lines were down.

I also didn't consider breaking a window and climbing through it to freedom to be a reasonable course of action, unless, of course, I wound up stuck inside for weeks and was running out of food. Replacing the glass could take forever, thus rendering the house uninhabitable. Been there, done that in Napaskiak.

So, I improvised. Since I had electrical power, I plugged in my hair dryer and used the heat from it to melt the ice. Then, I employed a kitchen knife to hack my way through the ice that remained. This effort took several hours, but I finally triumphed on Sunday.

I was really glad that I didn't have to wait for someone from the school to send out a search party for me on Monday morning.

Needless to say, it was a memorable weekend!

If you've never experienced a "whiteout," let me tell you that it's a potentially deadly situation if you ever have the misfortune of being caught outside in one. If you actually survive a white-out—translation: someone finds you before you, having become disoriented and blinded by the dense falling snow, and have wandered off into the vast, unpopulated expanses of tundra that surround most villages and towns in Alaska—you feel humbled by the power of Mother Nature and the vagaries of Fate.

You also experience a level of gratitude that's very difficult to describe. More often than not, your emotions send you to your knees to thank God for your salvation.

Although warnings of whiteout conditions were routinely broadcast on local radio stations, it's easy to miss one if you've hurriedly bathed and dressed before setting out early for school. I was one of a small group of teachers who arrived at school earlier than usual one morning only to discover that classes had been cancelled by the school district because of the blizzard.

Several of us remained at school until lunchtime, doing catch-up work and lesson plans in our empty classrooms at the request of the principal, who promised to treat us to lunch at a nearby restaurant as a thank you for our dedication to the students. Everyone gathered for lunch, fashioning a lead line with a rope so that no one would become lost during the trek to the restaurant.

I felt reluctant to play follow the leader in the midst of a whiteout, so I returned to my classroom and thought about my options. I finally decided to make my way home, a scant few blocks from the school.

To put it simply, I became lost within a matter of minutes. I wandered around, praying that I would stumble over a building or a vehicle within which I could take shelter. Didn't happen!

Instead, I continued to wander in ever expanding circles for quite some time, along the way growing more and more disoriented and frightened that I would die courtesy of my own stupidity. God took pity on me that day in the form of a man on a snowmobile, who rescued me from my hapless wandering and took me to my house.

Before I thanked my rescuer and said good-bye, he told me that I'd made it to the outskirts of town and would have been lost forever if he hadn't come upon me when he had.

At the end of the school year, I received formal notification that I'd been retained by the Northwest Arctic Borough School District and would be invited back to teach in September. I was happy about my retention, but I immediately began lobbying for a reprieve from another year at the middle school.

Having heard about a second grade teaching position at the Kotzebue Elementary School, I approached Mr. Sampson, the principal, and asked if I could apply for the job. The middle school principal resisted all of my efforts to relocate to a new school. In the end, Mr. Sampson, who seemed genuinely angry that my former principal tried to interfere with my transfer to the elementary school, became my advocate.

I will always be grateful to Mr. Sampson, in particular for his kindness and his support of my efforts to change schools. Teaching at the elementary school was very rewarding, despite the fact that I didn't work with Special Education students that year. I truly enjoyed the eagerness to learn reflected in the faces and attitudes of my second grade students.

When I was notified that I would have to move out of my little

Kotzebue students.

geodesic house, because it was being placed on the market for re-sale, I was disappointed. Despite its many flaws, I'd enjoyed the privacy of living there.

I'd made friends with another teacher, Dorothy, during one of the many Kotzebue whiteouts. One thing led to another, and we decided to become roommates when she learned that I would have to find new lodgings. I moved into her spare bedroom in the spacious home that she rented from a local minister.

To say that Dorothy possessed a difficult personality is a kind-ness. Although she was married to a carpenter, she didn't live with her husband. Her three children—two sons and a daughter—were grown and living far from home, each one pursuing life in other parts of the world.

Despite my mature years, Dorothy behaved like a devoutly reli-gious parent. She monitored my phone calls, often refusing to in-form me when someone wanted to speak to me. She fussed over my health, decided I suffered from lupus, and fretted loudly that I ate all the wrong foods.

Dorothy constantly reminded me of her "house rules," which in-cluded no drinking, no smoking, no male visitors, and absolutely no children in her house. The latter rule was the most frustrating, especially since my students liked to visit me after school hours.

Dorothy made the arbitrary decision to raise our rental fee, because she felt that the minister who owned our house wasn't receiving sufficient compensation from us. My only option, given the paucity of housing in Kotzebue, was to grind my teeth and endure. *I can do this!* became my personal mantra.

Eighteen

Although teaching elementary school children was an incredible treat after what I'd endured at the Kotzebue Middle School, it didn't mean that I was exempt from the community issues, both positive and negative, that arose in the school district.

There was an escalating concern among the teachers and school administrators about the high percentage of unmarried teenage girls who were becoming pregnant and adding their names to the welfare culture. We all believed that their thoughtless behavior, and the babies they subsequently delivered, threatened to dominate and, ultimately, undermine the Native population.

Cultural differences aside, there existed a genuine threat to the viability of the Native peoples, who persisted in resisting the realities of the contemporary world. The local college hosted an open forum one evening, during which interested teachers, medical personnel, and other community members were encouraged to air their concerns.

However, what began as a civil discussion among reasonable adults, soon deteriorated into a white versus Native confrontation when the subject of the high birth rate of illegitimate children was raised. A half-Native teacher, who was cohabiting with a local Native woman with whom he'd had two children and was expecting a third, took exception to the subject matter.

He insisted, "It's no one's business how we conduct our personal affairs. It is our right to remain unmarried and still have children. Unlike the white world, there's no stigma attached to a child who is born illegitimate. If the white teachers disapprove of our actions and our culture, then they can pack up and leave Kotzebue. We will not miss them and their interference."

A nurse in the audience responded to him, assuring the teacher that, as far as she was concerned, the high birth rate wasn't a moral issue, but a practical, medical one. The high rate of sexually transmitted diseases—some potentially deadly like AIDS—among the sexually active teens, she explained, contained the promise of Native population annihilation, not the maintenance of the status quo or an expansion of the population.

A teacher in the audience then chimed in with the comment, "It's not all right for you to tell us to mind our own business, because every person who pays taxes has a right to ask, 'who is supporting these babies?' Caring for a child is an expensive proposition when you consider the cost of the welfare programs and food stamps that are supporting these children." She went on to express her resentment that her tax dollars found their way into the pockets of irresponsible people who indiscriminately gave birth to children and then expected others to support and feed them.

I shared her opinion, although I didn't participate in the increasingly heated discussion as it unfolded. Many of the Native parents departed the forum, their anger and resentment evident.

Instead, I listened quietly to all of the speakers, attempting to figure out ways in which I could encourage my students to always be responsible for the choices they would make in their lives. Yes, they were still very young, but I was convinced that they could be taught to make wise choices and still display respect for their culture.

Sadly, even the youngest children, when encouraged to work hard in order to be rewarded, very innocently explained to me that hard work and a job weren't really necessary, since they could also collect welfare checks when they needed money—just like their parents.

Another speaker at the forum summarized the frustration felt by the majority of the white teachers and medical community personnel in Kotzebue when he said, "The Native peoples may love babies, but as soon as these children can walk unassisted, they are left to their own devices. We see these children arrive at school in mismatched clothing, without hats, mittens, and boots for warmth in the winter months.

"They are rarely ever fed a decent breakfast. In my world, having a child means taking responsibility for that child's well-being. It doesn't mean neglecting the child, because that same child will turn around in fifteen or twenty years and repeat that same neglect with the children he or she brings into the world."

Life lesson: one generation is the role model for the next generation.

What each person does or doesn't do really counts in the broader scheme of living and life. That was a memorable day from a personal perspective. In the aftermath of the heated exchanges that had taken place during the open forum, I redoubled my efforts to be the best possible role model for my students and to teach them the value of a life lived with dignity and honor.

———

My second grade students were a true blessing in many respects. The children that I taught were almost all Native Alaskans.

I constantly bragged about them, and know that I probably drove my fellow teachers crazy in the bargain.

But they really were terrific kids, despite the fact that the majority of them came from homes with serious alcohol related problems. Yes, their behavior could sometimes be very erratic, especially if they acted out as a result of a bad experience at home. Some faced the constant threat of being removed from parental custody by Children's Services.

I learned yet another valuable lesson when dealing with an endangered child. Even the smallest victims will instinctively resist being removed from the familiarity of their homes so that they can be protected against incest or violence. It doesn't matter to these children that this is the only way in which to safeguard them from further harm. What matters to them is what is familiar, not necessarily what is safest for them.

Several of my students were so neglected, it made my heart ache. I made every effort to treat each child as an individual, to show them the respect they deserved, and to listen to them when they confided in me.

There were isolated incidents that occurred which forced me to call in the legal authorities and protective services, but even those attempts to help often backfired, causing greater harm to the child and alienating them from me, their teacher and confidante, the one person they needed to be able to trust. At the risk of sounding as though I'm guilty of unfair stereotyping, my seven and eight-year-old Native students were forced to deal with all of the tragic family dysfunctions experienced by anyone growing up amidst alcohol-influenced poverty and violence.

Kotzebue was a "damp" village. By that, I mean that alcoholic beverages could not be sold within the city limits, although the possession of an alcoholic beverage within one's home was not prohibited.

Many people transported wine and hard alcohol into Kotzebue, either by air or by barge. Also, there was a complex network of resources for the dedicated alcoholics of Kotzebue. Committed drinkers can almost always locate a source of booze, even when it means using money that should be spent on food for their children.

"The Eskimo has fifty-two names for snow, because it is important to them; there ought to be as many for love."

Margaret Atwood

Nineteen

I rarely traveled during the school year, but I made an exception that winter when I decided to get away for a long weekend. I'd been feeling depressed and lonely, and I needed a change of pace. The cost of flying to Anchorage was too high for a brief weekend trip. So, I arranged to travel to Nome, a community on the Bering Sea that's quite famous as the final destination of the annual Iditarod Dogsled Race.

Nome swells to beyond its normal capacity every March for the conclusion of the Iditarod Race. Visitors and local residents greet the "mushers" with cheers, whistles, and camera flashes when they reach the finish line on the main street of the community. Celebrations ensue, the town's hotels, restaurants, and bars overflowing with revelers.

More than thirty-five hundred people reside year round in Nome. A little more than half of the population is Native. A transportation hub and commerce center for the area, Nome first made history in the late 1800s when miners discovered gold, and later as a result of the natural oil reserves beneath the surface of the surrounding terrain.

Visitors to Nome discover a wealth of carved ivory and other

Eskimo artifacts in the various retail shops. Commercial fishing, mining, a well-developed reindeer industry, and Native arts and crafts form the foundation income generated by the locals.

At that time, Nome claimed to house twelve churches and an equal number of bars, as well as several outpatient medical clinics, a major hospital, dental clinics, pharmacies, and several physicians. Like Kotzebue, one reaches Nome solely by air or barge.

Finish line of the Iditarod sled dog race in Nome.

Snowfall is extremely heavy during the winter season, which is also a time of extended darkness—usually from November until sometime in late February or early March. Alcohol is unrestricted in Nome, so the bars do a booming business regardless of the time of the day or night.

I decided to reserve accommodations at the Oceanwaves Bed and Breakfast in Nome. Having never visited the area, I knew no one who lived there, but that didn't dampen my growing excitement as I packed for this new adventure.

I'd heard wild stories about both the city of Nome and the Board of Trade Bar, the latter rumored to be one of the wildest establishments in all of Alaska and the Lower Forty-Eight. At one time, the legendary Nome brothels, notorious for the flamboyant women and men who frequented their beds, were as successful as the bars.

I flew out of Kotzebue aboard a commercial flight to Nome on a Friday night. An airport taxi delivered me to the Oceanwaves Bed and Breakfast, where I was greeted by the friendly owner and shown to my room.

After a good night's sleep, I set out the next morning to explore the area. I went shopping, enjoying the selections available to customers in the various retail establishments, visited a local museum to indulge my historical curiosity, and then purchased a map so that I wouldn't get lost when I wandered about town during the weekend.

I met Steve while having a drink in a local bar. An amputee, he still managed to live a full life with the aid of a steel prosthetic leg. An excursion to Little Diomede, allegedly one of the coldest places on the planet and a scant 25 miles from Russia, followed our meeting after I learned that there was an extra seat on the aircraft assigned to his tour group.

Little Diomede—not to be confused with the Russian Big Diomede—is situated on the Bering Strait, approximately one hundred and thirty-five miles from the community of Nome. The

International Date Line is about a mile and a half from Little Diomede and located between the two islands.

The village occupies about two square miles of high bluffs that are strewn with volcanic rock all the way down to sea level. Ninety percent of the one hundred and thirty people who reside on Little Diomede are Native. Their economy subsists on fish, crab, polar bears, and whales they harvest in order to guarantee their survival.

Little Diomede.

One reaches Little Diomede by boat or a small plane, but both modes of transportation pose numerous hazards to the passengers. Our small plane touched down on the ice in the midst of a bona fide blizzard. Thus, our trek to the village was accomplished slowly in below zero temperatures and gale force winds pummeling our bodies like angry fists.

Steve, my companion on this adventure, moved slower than most of our fellow passengers thanks to the unevenness of the terrain. Nonetheless, he managed to make his way over the frozen ground, across the snowdrifts, and up the many steps we had to climb to reach the hilltop village. In truth, we steadied each other as we walked, stumbled, slipped, stumbled some more, and then climbed an endless flight of stairs.

We browsed through the wares available in a small home tourist shop, where several of our tour companions purchased jewelry, ivory ornaments, and various other crafts and artifacts created or collected by the villagers. When it began to grow dark outside, we all carefully made our way down the stairs to the ice runway on

Main Street in Nome.

which our small plane awaited us. A local man kindly provided a sled to safely transport Steve to the aircraft.

After indulging myself with a hair styling appointment and a manicure once we arrived back in Nome, I returned to the bed and breakfast to change for the evening. A taxi took me to a local dance hall and bar, which boasted a band and singer. I joined a group of unattached women at their table for a drink, danced with several men, and met an FAA (Federal Aviation Administration) employee nicknamed "Miner." When he offered to show me the nightlife of Nome, I accepted his invitation.

We toured a variety of bars, dancing and laughing as the night unfolded. Miner's popularity was evident as he introduced me to, and was enthusiastically welcomed by, friends wherever we went.

By four in the morning, however, my feet hurt and I was exhausted, so I decided to return to the bed and breakfast. Late that next morning, I packed my luggage, settled my bill with the bed and breakfast owner, and joined Miner for brunch at a local restaurant. Afterwards, Miner loaded up my luggage and drove me to the airport, promising to be in touch with me in the future. He often traveled to Kotzebue for his work with the FAA.

All in all, the weekend was exactly what I needed to improve my spirits. When I arrived back in Kotzebue that afternoon, I felt better able to cope with the ever-meddling Dorothy, the bitterly cold Arctic climate, and the seemingly unceasing darkness of the winter months.

I did hear from Miner once I returned to Kotzebue, but he turned out to be less than reliable in the dating department. Although he'd make dates with me, he didn't show up for them. I grew exasperated with his rudeness and put him out of my mind.

I visited Nome a second time with two teachers, Daisy and Kim. They insisted that I join them, even though we weren't all that well acquainted. I caved in and agreed to make my second weekend trip. I had good memories of Nome, so it seemed somewhat karmic that I'd be visiting the area again in such a relatively short period of time.

Miner offered his apartment for our use that weekend. We accepted, all of us glad to be able to avoid the cost of lodging. He even managed to show up on time to drive us to the Kotzebue Airport, since he was temporarily working in the area.

I'm not altogether sure as to why, but neither Miner nor I acknowledged the fact that we'd met during my first weekend visit to Nome. It was as though we had this silent agreement, and we both intended to honor it.

A very pleasant and attractive co-worker of Miner's collected us at the airport and drove us to his apartment building. We were reduced to a state of stunned silence as we caught our first glimpse of the disaster zone that Miner called home. The place was revolting and virtually uninhabitable.

Totally disgusted, we decided to go out for supper. Kim introduced me to Reed at the legendary Pioneer Bar. He wore a white parka with wolf trim and was tall and thin. With a ready smile, Reed easily engaged us in conversation. After he told us that he was responsible for organizing the Bering Sea Golf Tournament, which was played on the ice, we helped him distribute the trophies to the teams that had represented the various Nome bars.

Three cleaning ladies of Nome.

Although my two companions pleaded fatigue and took a taxi back to Miner's apartment to stay for the night in their sleeping bags, I remained with Reed. We were happily swept along by the partying revelers who seemed to dominate Nome. Much later, I learned that Reed arranged to donate a substantial percentage of the golf tournament proceeds for academic scholarships and to the Rotary Club.

The next day, Kim, Daisy and I concocted a crazy tale about being the "cleaning ladies from Kotzebue," whom Miner had hired to sanitize his filthy apartment. That story provoked a great deal of good humor wherever we went, along with constant offers of drinks and employment by the many unattached men we encountered during the remainder of the weekend.

———

Upon our return to Kotzebue, Dorothy seemed eager to hear the details of our weekend in Nome. I regaled her with tales of all of the quirky personalities we'd encountered and the condition of Miner's apartment.

I did not, however, mention the bars we'd frequented or the all-night partying and dancing we'd enjoyed.

For some inexplicable reason, Dorothy was convinced that I'd met Mr. Right during the weekend in Nome. She wasn't exactly correct in her conclusion, but then she wasn't totally wrong, either.

After all, I'd met Reed, Miner's friend and a fellow FAA employee, in Nome. And like nearly every other man I'd become involved with in my less than sterling dating life, I should have been able to predict his M.O. (Mode of Operation) the instant I met him—he was gregarious, humorous, conversant on a myriad of topics, generous-natured, and, sadly, an alcoholic.

We saw a lot of each other, since his work with the FAA brought him to Kotzebue quite often. As we became better acquainted I also met several of Reed's friends. His inclination to socialize, as well as his high profile life in Nome courtesy of his Bering Sea Golf Tournament activities, translated into a constant whirlwind of activities and an excessive amount of alcohol consumption that grew somewhat off-putting as time passed.

Not all of my friends in Kotzebue liked Reed. I defended him, of course. How could I not defend the man with whom I was involved? I pointed out that he went out of his way to perform a vast array of favors for many of my friends, and he was generally good-natured and possessed a wickedly funny sense of humor. My friends, however, remained reluctant to be charmed by him or to accept him as the current man in my life. As far as they were concerned, Reed spelled trouble and disappointment for me.

More disturbed than I wanted to admit by their resistance to Reed, I eventually sought out the advice and counsel of a psychiatrist friend. She assured me that there was nothing wrong with me or my taste in men. According to her, men like Reed—men inclined to excess in nearly all aspects of their lives—dominated the planet. I welcomed her reassurance, using it as justification to continue dating Reed.

With the benefit of the passage of time and the kind of hindsight we all experience as we mature, I'm not altogether certain that I really—down deep in my heart—believed her reassurances at the time, but I wanted to in order to soothe my pride.

Bottom line: my taste in men wasn't the best.

Eventually, Reed spent less and less time in Kotzebue. As a result, he spent less and less time with me. I finally concluded that our relationship was either on indefinite hold or in its death throes.

You can imagine then how surprised I was when Reed called and proceeded to invite me to attend the Nome Rotary Club Annual Ball. At first, I was genuinely reluctant to accept his invitation. But when I learned that he'd also invited Kim and Daisy, the other two members of the infamous Nome "cleaning lady" crew, I accepted his invitation to attend Nome's pre-eminent social event of the season.

We took a commercial flight to Nome that weekend, subsequently settling in at Reed's apartment in order to prepare for the ball. With our party dresses, we were forced to wear snow pants and heavy boots. This looked a little odd but we weren't the only women dressed like this. The evening unfolded in an unexpected manner, however, and I was left sobered by the reality check administered to me.

Reed, who'd seemed very gracious and attentive at the outset of our time together that night, grew increasingly aloof as the hours passed. Finally, I realized that he had never had any intention of acting as my date for the evening.

Feeling upset by his behavior, I decided to abandon him at one of the watering holes we visited after the ball concluded. I relaxed and spent the balance of the night bar-hopping and dancing with friends, some old and some new. Truthfully, I had a much better time once Reed was no longer a part of the festivities.

When Daisy, Kim, and I finally returned to his apartment in the pre-dawn hours, Reed was sprawled across his bed, snoring loudly. It was just as well, I decided. As things turned out, I didn't hear from him again for a very long time. Our romance, at least what there was of it, was officially at a close. I actually felt relieved.

———

As the academic year ended, many of the teachers who'd experienced one conflict after another with the administrative personnel and school board members in charge of the Northwest Arctic Borough School District, not to mention being subjected to a wage freeze, decided to terminate their employment. Their reasoning was that a large number of departures would force the school district to unfreeze wages. They also believed that a group resignation would demonstrate their value, force the school district to rehire them, and strengthen their bargaining position during future disputes.

I participated, quitting along with everyone else even though I liked my work at the elementary school. I never imagined that the school district wouldn't see the error of its ways and ask us all to return.

Daisy and Kim, who'd declined to resign, repeatedly tried to persuade me not to behave precipitously. They urged patience so that the situation could be sorted out in a calm manner, but I refused to heed their advice.

After I tendered my resignation, the wages were unfrozen and all of the teachers who had remained loyal to the school district received salary increases. With the benefit of hindsight, I regretted my decision to end my relationship with the Northwest Arctic Borough School District. I even petitioned the principal of my school, asking him to consider rehiring me, but I was informed that my teaching position had already been filled.

Life lessons: turning back the clock isn't always possible, and, ultimately, we stand or fall on the choices we make. Playing follow the leader is a child's game.

———

After giving notice to my current roommate and quasi-landlord, Dorothy, making a good faith attempt to settle all my outstanding bills, and then packing my belongings, I departed Kotzebue for Anchorage.

I'd arranged temporary lodging with the acquaintance of a friend. My new landlady was a recent divorcee. She owned a spacious duplex and had received a large monetary settlement when she had divorced, so she initially appeared to be in a secure economic position.

The ultimate control freak, my landlady fretted constantly about the cost of everything under the sun. She even refused to heat my basement apartment. I felt so uncomfortable while I lived there that I used any excuse I could think of for not going home until the last possible moment each evening. I was relieved when I was finally able to move out of that frigid basement apartment.

Twenty

In need of a complete change of pace and with time on my hands, I set out on an adventure during the summer of 1991 in my ten-year-old, yellow Plymouth Duster with a slant six cylinder motor. My ultimate destination was Southern California, with several stops planned while I was in transit.

Despite the rust, the corrosion, the crumpled bumpers, the front headlight that hung from a strand of wire, a trunk that wouldn't open, and the hole in the interior floor of the vehicle, I loved that old Duster. She might have looked like an aging streetwalker, but I trusted her powerful engine almost more than I trusted myself.

Although everyone I knew counseled against the trip, citing the seemingly unreliable condition of my Duster, I ignored all the voices of doom. The trip did entail a certain amount of "doom," I'm sorry to say, but I still managed to reach my destinations of Vancouver, San Francisco, and then Southern California, regardless of the breakdowns and other mishaps I experienced.

During one stop to visit old friends, I managed to lock myself out of their house. My luggage and purse were inside. Their neighbor took great exception to my search for a hidden house key among the potted plants and lawn furniture. After threatening to call the police, the neighbor disappeared back inside his own home without any offer of hospitality.

My friends eventually arrived home, but not until well after midnight. I had spent the intervening hours not so happily cooling my heels in the rattletrap Duster.

On another occasion, this time in Southern California, a police officer pulled me over to the side of the road and requested both my driver's license and proof of insurance. The female officer couldn't quite believe that I'd driven the old Duster all the way from Alaska. She very nearly cited me for several vehicular irregularities, not the least of which was the absence of a tiny light that would illuminate my license plate. In the end, however, she took pity on me and sent me on my way, saying, "Drive carefully, and enjoy your stay in California."

When the gas gauge stopped functioning, I grew frustrated by the need to log every mile so that I wouldn't run out of gas without warning after filling the gas tank. When I inquired about the cost of a new gas gauge, it seemed unreasonably high.

That's when I decided, much to everyone's amusement, to write a personal letter to Lee Iacocca. I sought his advice on how to secure a new body for the Duster. That slant six cylinder motor was a winner, at least to my way of thinking, and I didn't want to give up on the vehicle without at least an attempt to salvage the situation. I also should have asked Mr. Iacocca if he was still single. Isn't hindsight wonderful!

Lee Iacocca answered my letter, providing me with all kinds of helpful advice. Everyone seemed amazed, but I wasn't surprised that he'd taken the time to respond to me. He was just that kind of a man. I also had a history of receiving responses from the unlikeliest of people and organizations, such as the Prime Minister of Canada, various international airlines, Congressmen, and clothing manufacturers.

As things turned out, I wound up leaving the old Duster behind when I departed California. I felt as though I'd abandoned a close friend as I left that day for the airport, but I couldn't ignore the reality that the odds were stacked against me of making a successful return trip to Alaska without major problems with the car.

My old friend Sam Stevens subsequently sold the car for me, but he informed me that the contents of the trunk had also gone to the new owner. Since the locked trunk contained a memento from my father—a shovel, believe it or not—I attempted to reclaim the item.

I finally did get that old shovel back, but it took a very long time, a pleading letter from me to the new owner of the Duster, and temporary storage in a friend's garage before Sam and his wife visited me in Alaska and personally delivered it to me. The shovel now stands in a place of honor in my garage.

Once I returned to Anchorage, I walked or used public transportation to get around town for quite some time. But with the advent of inclement weather just around the corner, I knew I couldn't delay the purchase of another vehicle for much longer.

A friend accompanied me on my quest to find the perfect used car—a car that would be as reliable as the Duster had once been. My friend had worked on the pipeline, and I believed his claim that he was quite well-versed in all things mechanical. It didn't take me long to figure out that even a superior mechanical mind can be seduced by a top-notch con job.

I decided on a pre-owned red Ford Escort with an odometer reading of 100,000 miles that was on display at a used car lot on Old Seward Highway. After an inspection of the engine by my mechanically oriented friend and a phone call to the former owner of the car, allegedly an Alaska Airlines flight attendant—she declared that she hadn't had any trouble with the car and that I could count on the used car dealer not to try and pawn off a lemon on me—I purchased the vehicle.

My problems with that blasted car commenced immediately upon driving out of the parking lot. I had a flat tire after less than two blocks of driving. A frantic call to that same dealership for assistance made it clear to me that I was on my own.

A service station mechanic dealt with the nail in the car's tire, patching it and declaring the car "as good as new." Not hardly!

The true nature of the lemon I was driving had yet to be revealed to me. The red Ford Escort broke down constantly. Even the local crop of tow truck drivers finally refused to respond to my requests for assistance. One said, "Don't call me again. That car would get stuck on wet grass."

———

Because I was unemployed, I made plans to join two female acquaintances for a trip to Dawson City in the Yukon Territory. I would then take a side trip to Fairbanks for the Alaska Teacher Job Fair while in transit back to Anchorage, since I would be driving my own car. Donna and Jan made the journey in their vehicle. I whispered a silent prayer that the Escort wouldn't fail me, and we set off on what I hoped would be a grand adventure.

Somewhere near the miniscule berg of Chicken—yes, that's the name of a community—my Ford Escort died. As I guided the car to the side of the road, I no longer wondered if I'd been crazy to trust the Escort on such a long trip. The truth of my misplaced optimism could no longer be denied.

Donna and Jan turned around when they saw me come to a

stop. They pulled up behind my Escort at the edge of the road. Before too much time passed, a series of well-intentioned men, who drove every make and model of vehicle under the sun, stopped to offer assistance. Each man proceeded to diagnose and then attempt to repair the problem.

Assorted families also pulled off the road and joined in the confusion. They spilled out of their RV's and station wagons, the children picking berries from the bushes at the side of the road while the women gathered in clumps and gossiped as their men discussed the finer points of car engine problems. It was like watching the evolution of a three-ring circus.

When all of my would-be rescuers failed to fix the problem, I finally called a tow truck service and had the Escort taken into the small village of Tok. The diagnosis by the local mechanic: a cracked engine block. I made a useless and very angry call to the used car dealership that had sold me the car in Anchorage, but it was a Sunday and no one answered the telephone. I wound up leaving a voice mail, which did little to mute my rage at having been so royally hoodwinked.

Jan, Donna, and I continued on to Dawson. Tension grew with every passing mile, and it persisted even after we reached the rain-soaked community of Dawson and the hotel we'd booked. Although we occasionally dined together or went out to gamble, we each went our own way during the majority of the time we spent there.

We finally drove back to Tok, learning upon our arrival that my Ford Escort wasn't yet repaired. Donna and Jan put their heads together. They offered to drive me to the job fair in Fairbanks, provided I volunteered to pay for our gas. Of course, I agreed to their request, and also paid for some of our meals. To be blunt, I was really surprised by their kindness, considering the amount of tension that had flowed among us.

The Alaska Teacher Job Fair failed to meet any of my expectations. I responded positively to a subsequent invitation to be interviewed, along with another candidate, by the Yukon Flats School District, but the interview by the Native board members turned into a version of Chinese water torture. Neither I nor the other candidate was offered the position of reading teacher at Fort Yukon.

We weren't told why we'd both been turned down, so I contacted the Superintendent to learn the truth. As it turned out, one of my former colleagues from Kotzebue interviewed with the Fort Yukon school board shortly after we left. He was offered and accepted the position, but he didn't complete an entire school year. However small it might sound, I must confess to feeling vindicated in my belief that the Yukon Flats School District had made a serious mistake by not hiring me.

Although I interviewed for a few other teaching positions, there were no employment offers forthcoming. So, I returned to Anchorage and temporarily took up residence in the little house I still owned since my tenants were scheduled to move out.

I didn't stay long at my house, deciding instead to find new tenants to support the mortgage. I rented a room from a friend in order to conserve my funds.

"A woman can do anything.
She can be traditionally feminine; she can work, she can stay
at home; she can be aggressive, she can be passive;
she can be any way she wants with a man.
But whenever there are the kinds of choices there are today,
unless you have some solid base, life can be frightening."
Barbara Walters

Twenty-One

By the time I applied for a teaching position in 1991 on the island of Kauai in Hawaii, I was in desperate financial straits and on the verge of having to find yet another new place to live. Special Education teachers were in great demand in Hawaii. So, I immediately mailed off my résumé.

The Kauai School District contacted me more quickly than I would have ever expected and conducted the interview over the phone. I consoled myself with the thought that living in the islands would be a temporary interlude—a working vacation—and that I could return to Anchorage at the close of the upcoming school year. By then, perhaps I would have been offered a teaching position in Alaska.

Although I had also filed several applications with the various school districts in and around Anchorage, nothing had occurred to offer me any hope of local employment. Several weeks later, the Kauai School District contacted me again. Their representative insisted that I immediately depart for the island if I still wanted the Special Education teaching position. Otherwise, they indicated that they would withdraw their offer of employment.

I took the required leap of faith and prepared for an imminent departure from Anchorage. Following a going away party given by several friends, I flew via Seattle to Honolulu. From there I boarded a connecting flight to the island of Kauai.

The principal of the school where I was scheduled to teach was supposed to meet my flight. She left me waiting at the Lihue Airport for a long time. When she finally arrived, her attitude made it clear that I was nothing more than an inconvenience she had to bear—an unwelcome white teacher forced upon her by the school district.

I ignored her hostility, staying so briefly at her home while I arranged for a place to live and a used car to purchase, that she was obviously shocked by my speedy departure from her so-called hospitality.

I moved into top floor accommodations at a bed and breakfast inn in Koloa the next day. Operated by a former teacher, the lack of guests at the bed and breakfast benefited me. I truly enjoyed the beautifully decorated Japanese motif of the small studio apartment.

Marissa, the owner of the bed and breakfast, tried to be hospitable, but the presence of her live-in boyfriend, who was friendly to every woman he encountered, caused a certain amount of friction. To be blunt, Marissa displayed her insecurity and jealousy on a daily basis. My best option, I quickly decided, was to steer clear of both of them whenever possible.

Kauai, known as the Garden Island, is extraordinarily beautiful. A less developed island than Maui, visitors to Kauai can walk endless miles of beach, explore rain forests, or observe the gardens of Kauai's residents. The island is small, approximately twenty-five miles long and thirty-three miles wide.

The tiny hamlet of Hanalei, which is situated on the north shore of the island, is exquisite. Private homes and a few five star resorts are tucked in among the towering fir trees and the lush tropical vegetation that hugs the coastline. The road stops at the northern edge of the island a few miles past Hanalei. Dramatic cliffs, the backdrop of the Na Pali Coastal region, provide limitless views of the Pacific Ocean.

Multi-hued wildflowers cover the landscape of the island in the spring. Waialua Falls also provides a spectacular example of tropical lushness and a tumultuous waterfall that drops more than eighty feet into the canyon below.

Life on Kauai couldn't have been more different than Alaska. I was totally unprepared for the constant rain and the presence of every type of insect imaginable, especially during the fall and winter months. There were many times when I would have happily traded island life for a bug free, dark Arctic winter. I'm not kidding you one little bit!

Life lesson: paradise is a very subjective perception.

My students, who ranged in age from five to eighteen, were classified as EED, Extremely Emotionally Disturbed. Working with a total of thirty children—although my individual classes were usually composed of three to five students—as a Special Education teacher could not have been more difficult.

The majority of the younger students under my supervision were "drug babies." They shared many of the symptoms and behavioral problems of the fetal alcohol syndrome children whom I taught in Alaska. Although I was of the opinion that several of the children should have been diagnosed as LD, Learning Disabled, I knew that the school received additional funding when a child was categorized as EED.

Bottom line: I kept my opinions to myself.

Attempting to maintain control over, and teach, thirty Special

Education children on a daily basis is a daunting enough endeavor for any teacher. The overwhelming challenge of instructing over thirty of these children is not easy. Some are inclined to act up and act out at will, cannot always understand why they must behave with decorum and respect for others, and utilize violence as a means by which to assert themselves when they are frustrated or angry. This is the equivalent of trying to climb Mount Everest without the proper training, equipment, and a contingent of veteran Sherpa guides.

Yes, I possessed the experience, training, and certification as a Special Education teacher, but the sheer number of students for whom I was expected to take responsibility demoralized me.

I quickly concluded that the previous Special Education teacher had failed both the students and the school in terms of establishing discipline, structure, and clearly stated academic expectations. These expectations, considered a reasonable standard by most teachers and school administrators, are essential to facilitate even a modicum of success for children in a classroom setting, and they are generally enforced in most school environments.

To further complicate both my life and the lives of the children for whom I was responsible, I immediately saw signs of physical abuse and profound neglect among the students placed under my supervision. Not all of them were abused or neglected, of course, but there were sufficient numbers of obvious victims to arouse my instincts and my concern for their welfare.

The language skills of many of the students, as well as the principal and the majority of the Native Hawaiian teachers, resulted in a pigeon-style English that made my understanding of them very difficult at times. There were numerous occasions when it was impossible for me to grasp the actual verbal intent of particular students. Thus, I was forced to guess at the meaning of their attempts at dialogue with me.

Although I'd dealt with these same language use challenges among the Native population in the Alaska Bush, it wasn't to this degree. When faced with the improper use of the English language by fellow Kauai teachers with college degrees, I either asked for a translation into plain English (always with a smile on my face so as not to offend anyone), or I just bit my tongue to conceal my frustration with them.

Life lesson: Upon occasion, all you can do is punt!

———

Family crises routinely plagued many of my Special Education children, from the obvious neglect and abuse I observed on a daily basis, to the remarriage of parents and the resulting lack of adjustment by the child to the new family dynamic. In one particular case, a student, who had frequent temper tantrums, finally revealed that her father regularly beat her.

When Maude revealed the bruises and cuts on her legs, I followed the established procedure and sent her for an interview with the school psychologist. He was tasked with performing an evaluation and the subsequent handling of the problem.

The outraged psychologist immediately reported the battery of this child to the authorities, and the case was brought to the attention of the local District Attorney, who filed charges against Maude's father. I gave testimony at his trial, discovering while I was enmeshed in this tangled chain of events that Maude's father had a long history of beating and abusing her and her siblings. Until now, he'd only been cited for these offenses. I won't even comment on the enmity my actions and resulting courtroom testimony earned me from the principal and many of my fellow teachers.

—·—

Another difficulty that arose while I taught at the Kauai school involved the resistance and, often obvious, resentment by island teachers, who were primarily Native Hawaiian or Japanese Hawaiian, to white teachers. The only other Anglo on the staff and I were routinely ostracized.

The school principal did absolutely nothing to repair these cultural problems or to facilitate a better understanding of the situation by all of the teachers on staff. In fact, she often failed to include our names on the roster for meeting notices, and we were rarely invited to attend activities during our non-school hours.

I knew that I would be leaving at the end of the school year, so I felt confident that I could weather the reverse discrimination tactics of the principal and the other teachers until my departure. The other white teacher, however, had an even more challenging time, which culminated when she was not invited back to teach during the next school year. Her undeserved negative Teacher Evaluation made being hired by another school district that much more difficult for her to achieve, but she ultimately prevailed, thanks to her dedication and skill as a teacher.

The principal of the school made it her practice to ignore me. Even when other teachers offered complimentary statements to her about my Special Education students, the result of my efforts to improve their overall written and verbal communication skills, she refused to acknowledge their progress or my dedication to them. I mentally consigned her to the "stupid" category in my thoughts, and I privately renewed my resolve to continue to do my best for those students who depended upon me.

———·———

The Special Education students suffered the added indignity of being forced to occupy a storage room rather than a bona fide classroom. It seemed like the ultimate insult to me that my students and I shared space with stored containers of food utilized by the school cook for the lunchroom, stacks of chairs, miscellaneous boxes of school supplies, items of furniture not presently being used by the school staff, and assorted debris.

Add potential health risks to the existing insult of the environment of that storage room, especially when you consider the squadrons of cockroaches and the filth and mold encrusted walls we were forced to endure, and you've got a very clear picture of our daily circumstances.

My concern about the potential health consequences to myself and the students nibbled at the edge of my mind like an unwelcome battalion of termites the entire time I taught school in Kauai. Despite the passage of time, I doubt I'll ever forget the experience.

Much to my chagrin, I've learned during my years as an educator that insufficient attention is paid to the ideal learning environment for most Special Education children. In my case at the Kauai school, I was obviously handicapped from the start. In an effort to upgrade the negative ambiance of the store room/classroom, I tacked up posters on the walls after scrubbing them. The two large windows in the storeroom guaranteed a brightly lighted atmosphere, which stabilized our moods as we set to work each day, and the presence of a sink allowed us to wash when the need arose. Restroom facilities were in another building, but the children and I learned to adapt to that inconvenience.

The reward system—remember the sweets I gave to my Alaska Bush students—was one I had planned to utilize with my Special Education students in Hawaii. I arrived on the island with candy supplies packed in my luggage. However, candy of any kind was forbidden as a reward for the students by the Kauai school principal. As a result, I devised an alternative reward system by assembling a small cache of inexpensive watches, books, pencils, note pads, comb and brush sets for the girls, and other equally modest items.

Students in Kauai, Hawaii

Most of the students were excited at the prospect of being rewarded for their academic efforts. Although I considered the rewards a motivational tool, some of the other teachers frowned on what they felt was my effort to bribe my students.

Bottom line: Rewards were an effective tool! So I refuse to apologize to anyone for my tactics.

———

The incessant rain on the island of Kauai is a dominant feature of the winter months. The decrepit used car I'd purchased upon my arrival wasn't just filthy, it also leaked like a proverbial sieve.

I took to wearing a large plastic garbage bag as a poncho to keep my clothing dry when I drove that wreck of a car back and forth to school during the downpours of the wet winter months. I'm confident that the manufacturers of these plastic lawn cuttings and leaf disposal bags would be gratified to learn of my innovative use of their product.

Twenty-Two

One of the most spectacular natural settings on Kauai is the Waimea Canyon. It is approximately ten miles long, at least a mile wide, and plunges to a depth of 3,600 feet. This dramatic example of the result of thousands of years of rivers overflowing their banks and floods originating from Mount Waialeale rainy season provides fantastic views of Kalalau Valley. A rainbow of colors from the vegetation adorning the cliffs on either side of the canyon is overwhelming.

Mark Twain once remarked, "Waimea Canyon is the Grand Canyon of the Pacific Ocean." Like most people who've experienced the grandeur of the canyon, I applaud the accuracy of his comment.

Each time I viewed the canyon, the result of a long drive up a winding road to various lookout spots carved into the cliffs, I was entranced by the breathtaking majesty and beauty. I often fantasized about pitching a tent, settling in for the duration, and savoring the magical quality of the surrounding landscape and panoramic views.

However, that fantasy was destined to remain a fantasy, thanks primarily to the cost of living. Life on the island of Kauai proved to be far more expensive than I had ever imagined. Most people, and I include the principal and teachers at my school, were forced to take second and third jobs, their part-time employment supplementing their paychecks and allowing them to live modestly in a very costly environment.

Although I was offered a part-time position as a tutor that included accommodations, I declined the job. Now, I know what you're thinking: part-time employment would have helped to defray my expenses. At the time, however, the woman who sought to employ me complained bitterly about the inadequate schools on the island, along with indicting the competence of the tutors she'd previously engaged to assist her son.

I must admit that I was lonely enough and sufficiently strapped for funds at that point in time to seriously consider accepting her offer, but I reminded myself that I was on a working vacation, and that I'd long ago learned how to live simply and economically.

———

It took time for my solitary existence as The Lone Stranger to resolve itself, and I eventually made several friends. Because there were many other single men and women living and working on the island, some of us managed to become acquainted in the evenings during social outings to bars and restaurants, while grocery shopping, at ukulele get togethers like the Kanikapila Kakau, or while in line at the local movie theater.

We routinely congregated at nightspots and various bars, which were favored by the local residents. Additionally, we availed ourselves of the luxurious hotel and resort facilities that dotted the island. We chatted, danced, and indulged ourselves, often courtesy of a few drinks, by singing along with the bands in the lounges of the various hotels.

Tuesday nights became our weekly beach party night. Sitting around a blazing fire pit, talking, singing, or listening to a ukulele player, proved to be a wonderful change of pace from the grueling days of teaching and coping with the hostility of the principal. I dated casually while on the island of Kauai, but a long-term relationship wasn't in the cards for me.

———

With the prospect of an island Christmas ahead of me I decided to travel to California, which had been my habit in past years whenever I could manage the airfare. Since my bed and breakfast lodgings would not be available to me during the holidays, it made sense to pack and store my belongings, then make airline reservations.

I visited friends in Laguna Beach, California, but only after a nearly catastrophic event at the airport on the day of my departure. Fortunately, the purse I'd managed to misplace in the women's restroom at the Lihue Airport had been turned in to the owner of a small retail establishment, courtesy of an honest soul who didn't feel compelled to abscond with my airline tickets, money, identification, and credit cards.

We all know that that sort of honesty and kindness rarely happens in our "me-oriented" world, so I felt doubly blessed that day after locating my lost purse as I winged my way east across the Pacific to Southern California. Upon arriving in the Laguna Beach area, I relaxed, socialized with friends, and spent three wonderful weeks without the threat of rain, humidity, pesky insects, and geckos springing out of nowhere and landing on my head. Pure heaven!

My return to Kauai at the end of the Christmas holiday season signaled a permanent end to the lodging arrangement I'd enjoyed on the top floor of Marissa's bed and breakfast inn. After collecting my possessions and loading them into a car, I rented an expensive furnished condominium located a block from Poipu Beach.

The condo was situated in close proximity to several luxury resorts like the Hyatt and an abundance of time-shares and condominiums. The pristine white sands of Poipu Beach and the scented breezes offered a reprieve from the world, not to mention the kind of privacy I truly savored during the balance of my year on Kauai.

Yes, the condo was extremely expensive, far more costly than my teaching salary justified. I rationalized my decision to rent the place, and used funds from my savings each month to supplement the rent payment. I also turned into something of a vegetarian in order to cut back on grocery expenses, except when dining out with a date, of course. That's when I indulged my craving for a steak dinner.

Not far from my condominium was the Spouting Horn, a lava-formed, tube-shaped blowhole that shoots a spray of water fifty or more feet into the air. Visitors and locals alike take great delight in this natural phenomenon. Because the Spouting Horn was just one of many island tourist attractions, it was a simple matter to play tour guide to friends and relatives who visited me on the island of Kauai. When I wasn't conducting driving tours of the island, my guests also enjoyed long walks on the sparsely populated beaches or used the tennis courts at my condominium complex.

———

By the time the school year concluded and I had made arrangements to depart Kauai, I couldn't wait to board the aircraft that would return me to my beloved Alaska. While most people in this world are eager to visit Hawaii or to indulge in dreams of taking up residence on some tropical island, I am a diehard Alaskan.

The thought of returning to Anchorage dominated my every word, thought, and action during the final weeks of my stint as a teacher in Kauai. I was very grateful when I finally arrived in Anchorage.

Twenty-Three

Nuiqsut, 1992-1993

I settled briefly into my little house upon my arrival in Anchorage. There was no time to recover from the journey or to unpack, however. I immediately made arrangements to attend the Alaska Teacher Job Fair in Fairbanks.

It no longer mattered to me where I taught school in Alaska; I just wanted to teach. And, in order to become vested in the Alaska State Teachers' Retirement program, it was imperative that I maintain an active employment status for at least three more years.

The shortage of teaching positions in Alaska remained a problem. After several fruitless interviews and long weeks of worry, I secured an offer of temporary employment as a first grade teacher in the Bush village of Nuiqsut. I was informed that, until non-specific "problems" with the teacher I was to temporarily replace were resolved, I wouldn't be offered permanent employment in Nuiqsut.

Regardless of the uncertainty of a temporary teaching opportunity at Trapper School, I accepted the position and immediately began to prepare for an imminent departure. Had I not agreed to present myself to the school district before week's end, the offer would have been withdrawn. Two friends moved into my home to house-sit for me.

I made it as far as Prudhoe Bay, but unexpected blizzard conditions decreed that it would be impossible to proceed any further. All flight operations had to be cancelled because of the severe weather.

There is a seventy mile long ice road situated along the banks of the frozen Beaufort Sea from Prudhoe Bay to Nuiqsut, but that mode of travel was not an option for me thanks to the packed boxes and luggage that I'd brought along for my new start in Nuiqsut. I stayed at a local hotel until the weather conditions eased and flights into and out of Prudhoe Bay resumed.

———·———

Nuiqsut is a tiny Eskimo village situated on the banks of the Colville River. It occupies about nine square miles of terrain, and was one of three neighboring villages that were abandoned by the Native population in the late 1940s.

The federal government funded the rebuilding of Nuiqsut in 1973. Building materials were hauled in from Barrow, which was located one hundred and sixty miles to the west, by huge tractor-trailer rigs and powerful snow machines.

Approximately ninety families resided in Nuiqsut, with a base population of about four hundred and thirty-five. More than eighty percent of the local residents are Natives. As is the case in many Alaska Bush villages, the income derived by most of the residents is primarily subsistence level, but many earn supplemental funds by trapping, creating crafts, or hunting and fishing. Their normal diet consists of caribou, bowhead and beluga whales, polar bears, seal, moose, and miscellaneous types of fresh fish.

Purified water is transported to the village twice a week from a nearby lake. Many residences had a water tank. An added feature of village life is the fact that a sanitary disposal hauling service collects the honey buckets from homes and businesses.

Aircraft service, both commercial and private, for travel into and out of Nuiqsut is accomplished year round thanks to the snow machines that keep the runways clear of excess snow. When you consider the fact that the daily temperature is normally far below freezing and the snowfall is heavy for more than nine months of each year, an airport in this community is a true bonus for commerce, travelers, or those in need of emergency medical care that can't be provided in the village.

The November, 2000 production of oil from the Alpine Oil Field has changed the entire village with increased employment opportunities, and a natural gas pipeline into Nuiqsut promised to decrease the cost of operating diesel generators and home heating.

—•—

The school principal transported me to my new lodgings: the crowded dwelling of a woman whose husband was on leave in Anchorage. Since the lady of the house was out of town and there was little room for my possessions, I left everything packed except the perishable foods I'd brought with me. I crammed the food into an already crowded refrigerator and freezer.

Nervous about my first day as a teacher in Nuiqsut, I slept little that night. The next morning I made my way to the school. Thus began my trial by fire as the teacher who was responsible for, yet again, a very poorly behaved class of first graders.

You won't be at all surprised that I thought these kids were Special Education students, since discipline is a characteristic issue in their classrooms. When I said as much to the principal, he looked taken aback and replied that these children were just "your every-day first graders."

I was shocked and somewhat disheartened. And I couldn't help wondering if I'd ever be blessed with the opportunity to teach children who lacked aggressive tendencies that were both threatening and destructive. Self-pity threatened that morning, but I managed to push it aside in order to focus on the tasks at hand.

Nuiqsut students.

The Trapper School accommodated one hundred and fifty students during an average school year. The benefits, aside from the obvious academic ones, were immediately apparent to me when I learned that the children received both breakfast and lunch in the school cafeteria. For many of the students, these meals were the only ones they received each day.

Reading skills were among the few attributes possessed by these first graders—a nice counterpoint to their obvious behavioral and personality issues. Many of the children had begun their educations courtesy of the federally funded Head Start program, then a year of pre-school, and finally kindergarten. By the time they reached the first grade, most were experiencing their fourth year of schooling.

Not having to instruct my students in basic reading skills freed me up to focus on gaining control over them, which was an absolute must if I had a prayer of actually functioning as a teacher. Given the fact that the principal of the school routinely faulted those teachers who had disciplinary difficulties with their students, I knew the onus was on me to deal with these as soon as possible.

I had my work cut out for me as I coped with all manner of inappropriate behavior—from bullying tactics employed by the boys against the girls, who were a minority in the class, to overt acts of violence that set my teeth on edge and yielded bloodied noses and black eyes among the children when fights broke out. Temper tantrums and the destruction of desks, chairs, and school supplies contributed to the general mayhem.

It didn't take long at all for me to realize that the woman with whom I was sharing a house was also the spouse of the teacher I'd replaced—the same teacher who had been described by the principal as having "problems." Leah was cordial, but she was also very secretive about her husband's "problems." At first, I thought he had some fatal disease.

When Leah returned, we talked a little but she did not mention the conundrum. She said it was difficult for her to have a roommate because she hadn't shared with anyone since college. Because of the secrecy, I decided that her husband must have AIDS or maybe he'd had a heart attack, and she couldn't talk about it. Leah had a phone put in her room and would go there and talk quietly. She cried a lot and, with the dark days (the sun goes down for two months and you don't see it again until January), I was depressed.

I found out later from Leah that her husband was in jail for theft of school property. She made excuses for him but he had stolen some outdated computers, printers, and other school materials and sold them. Her husband did not come back, so I signed a contract to finish the year.

———

As I became better acquainted with several of my fellow teachers, and as a consequence of my own experience, I grew to dislike the school principal more and more with every passing month. He had one favorite instructor, a male teacher, whom he seemed to be grooming to be a principal.

Despite the achievements of the other teachers and the resulting positive strides being made by their students, the principal ignored his staff. I don't think that I ever heard a word of praise, for the students or the teachers, from him during his tenure as principal. If anything, he penalized them for the pettiest reasons.

The teaching staff was expected to participate in extracurricular activities for the students. From selling tickets at basketball games, chaperoning school dances, assisting in the library and computer lab, to managing a booth at the Halloween Carnival, we were all involved during what would normally be considered our off-duty hours.

Requesting an exemption from these extracurricular activities simply earned us the ire of the principal, so most of the teachers participated, albeit somewhat grudgingly at times. We were well compensated as teachers in Nuiqsut, and I suspect that almost everyone—I include myself in this group—felt, at least to some degree, that our salaries might have justified our additional duties.

———

Leah lived in fear that one of the villagers would exact revenge upon her as a result of her husband's behavior. When the house was broken into during our absence one weekend, she was convinced that this was a part of her penance for being married to a thief.

When I asked her why she remained loyal to him, she justified her decision to stay married to Robby with the explanation that they'd been together since her teenage years. Leah, a genuinely kind and generous-natured woman, had never been intimate with another man.

She clearly had a blind spot where her husband was concerned. To complicate matters even more, she'd lived her entire married life in a subservient role, acceding to Robby's wishes in all things. I honestly don't think she'd ever made a decision for herself, by herself. I felt both empathetic and frustrated with her perception of herself as a second-class citizen undeserving of equality in their marriage. I wondered how she could surrender her life and her identity to such a man.

I also couldn't help wondering if, once Leah and Robby were reunited at the conclusion of his two year prison sentence, she would have been on her own long enough to have sprouted some wings of independence. After all, she was now making decisions without her husband's approval for the first time in her adult life.

I harbored a secret optimism that she would tell him she wanted a divorce the next time he called her on the telephone from prison. Wishful thinking on my part, I know, but I confess to being an eternally optimistic soul who persists in wishing the underdog well.

Twenty-Four

When the school district determined that Robby would not be returning to teach in Nuiqsut, I was formally offered a contract to teach for the balance of the school year. I accepted the contract, of course.

In the final months of the school year I came to the conclusion that I had no desire to return to Nuiqsut. Although I'd made inroads with my students, I hadn't been able to create a comfortable rapport with the principal of the school, and I didn't think that he intended to retain me for the next school year. Rumor had it that he had employed a friend of his to take my position.

I decided to immediately seek employment for the upcoming school year, rather than wait to job hunt during summer break. I requested a few days off and teamed up with a fellow teacher, Roger, to attend the Alaska Teacher Job Fair in Anchorage. Despite several mishaps as we traveled by truck to Prudhoe Bay, Roger and I managed to make our way to Anchorage.

Despite our delayed arrival, the Job Fair proved to be the most promising one I'd ever attended, in part because I was repeatedly mistaken for a principal and interviewed for "principal" positions. My frustration was evident every time I endeavored to correct this misconception, and the school superintendents who interviewed me seemed very surprised.

Some of the interviewers found my Bush teaching experiences particularly entertaining. The fact that I possessed a Special Education teacher certificate helped me a great deal also.

In the end, I felt guardedly optimistic that I would be offered a viable teaching position as a result of attending the Teacher Job Fair. Roger, unfortunately, wasn't nearly as optimistic. He hadn't had many interviews and he didn't feel confident about his performance in the ones he'd had. Having endured very negative experiences at job fairs in the past, I felt compassion for him.

––·––

The return flight to Prudhoe Bay was uneventful until we began our descent and landed in the midst of a major blizzard. Our connecting flight to Nuiqsut in a very small private plane was grounded.

Our belongings were loaded onto a larger aircraft, one that the aviation authorities had determined to be more capable of making the short flight to Nuiqsut in spite of the tumultuous and extremely dangerous weather conditions. Despite the heavy snowfall, gusting winds, and sub-zero temperatures, Roger and I were delivered safely to Nuiqsut and we reclaimed our possessions in the midst of a whiteout that brought back memories of another whiteout experience that still gave me nightmares.

Before departing the Anchorage Teacher Job Fair, I'd registered with an agency that would take my phone calls and receive any correspondence from the various school districts that might be interested in hiring me. Considering the reasonable fee for this service and the remoteness of my location, it made sense to utilize their services.

Chapter 24

My decision to engage them proved to be a good one. One of their employees went above and beyond the call of duty on my behalf when inquiries began coming in from some of the school districts. Because of the kindness and extra effort of one of the agency's clerks, I received a telephone call regarding a teaching position in Nondalton.

The following day my principal in Nuiqsut spoke to the Nondalton principal. He confirmed my references and actually recommended me for employment in Nondalton. I later discovered that the two principals were acquainted.

When the Director of Special Education for the Lake and Peninsula Borough School District contacted me and formally offered me a teaching position, I was elated. I promptly accepted their offer.

My principal told anyone who would listen that he'd secured my new job for me. I had mixed feelings about his remarks, of course, since he'd declined to retain me for the upcoming school year. Yet another example of the man's arrogance, I decided.

For my part, I focused on more important issues, however, like the fact that I wouldn't have to live or teach under the critical gaze of a contrary school principal, who possessed all of the passive aggressive tendencies of a bona fide control freak. I would also be a year closer to becoming vested in the Alaska State Teachers' Retirement System. At the time, I had no idea just how challenging it would be to teach in Nondalton.

Roger, my colleague and traveling companion to the Alaska Teacher Job Fair in Anchorage, didn't receive any offers of employment. Fortunately for him, alternative employment became unnecessary. Roger was retained for the next school year in Nuiqsut by our very unpredictable principal.

As I prepared for my departure from Nuiqsut in 1993, I sold my extra food reserves and all of the other personal items that I no longer wanted or needed. Leah, my misguided housemate and fellow teacher, also prepared to depart the Bush village.

I couldn't help but wonder about Leah's possible fate, but I cautioned myself against counseling her to finally start thinking for herself and kept my thoughts unspoken. She, like the rest of us who occupy this planet, would have to navigate a successful path through her own doubts under her own steam, perhaps even reinvent herself along the way and create a new life for herself. I hoped she would do just that, but I wasn't overly optimistic.

As I made my way home to Anchorage, the thought of having a summer that wouldn't involve racing around like a crazy woman in search of her next job delighted me. As it turned out, I had a truly wonderful summer that year.

Twenty-Five

Nondalton, 1993-1995

Teaching in Nondalton was a mixed blessing. On one hand, I was gainfully employed and utilizing my Special Education credentials. But, on the other hand, the Nondalton teaching experience evolved into a test of who would survive the experience—me or the newly assigned principal of the school in which I taught.

Following in-service training for the upcoming school year, a time during which I became acquainted with several of my fellow teachers and Carrie, a school district traveling guidance counselor, we all made the journey to Nondalton. A Bush community situated on the western shore of Six Mile Lake, between Lake Clark and Iliamna Lake, Nondalton is located one hundred and ninety miles southwest of Anchorage.

The area of Nondalton encompasses approximately eight square miles of land and one square mile of water. It is accessible solely by aircraft. Nondalton is a Tanaina Indian name.

The village was once located on the northern shore of Six Mile Lake, but it was later relocated to the western shore. The population was less than two hundred people, most of whom are members of the Dena'ina Indian tribe. As in most remote Bush communities, the residents live a subsistence lifestyle, fishing in the numerous lakes and rivers located nearby.

Nondalton had a small grocery store, post office, medical clinic, and a relatively new Native Corporation complex. The latter building accommodates both the business and communal needs of the village and outlying areas, and for holding various festivals and other Native sponsored activities.

———

Teacher housing in Nondalton was humble. I moved into an old trailer that was badly in need of numerous repairs. Still, I voiced

My Nondalton home.

no complaint about the accommodations provided by the school district, and promised myself that I would initiate the appropriate improvements to assure a hospitable and comfortable environment for myself.

With two small bedrooms, a living and dining room, hot and

cold running water, and functional bathroom plumbing, I celebrated the fact that I hadn't been condemned to the use of a honey bucket again.

The heater, which was included in my monthly rental fee, worked. It compensated somewhat for the lack of insulation in the poorly constructed trailer. I purchased an electric space heater to guarantee an additional source of warmth during the arctic winter.

The furniture in the trailer could only be categorized as junk and qualified as worthy of placement in the local dump. But beggars can't be choosey, so I tolerated it.

My mattress in my bedroom bespoke the ingenuity of the previous resident—the bed sat upon large fruit cocktail cans because it lacked a proper metal frame. I exercised great caution when turning over at night in that bed—otherwise, it collapsed and pitched me directly onto the floor.

A spectacular view from the trailer compensated considerably for the shabby condition of my accommodations. Nondalton was quite lovely; picture-postcard scenic, in fact. The Chigmit Mountains towered majestically in the distance. In the spring months, the rugged terrain is blanketed with wildflowers, while in winter great masses of snow spill down in billowing clouds from one mountain peak or another.

———

It is my destiny to experience questionable relationships with the principals of the schools in which I teach. Nondalton offered no reprieve from this.

Harry Bartlett, the newly assigned school principal, as the result of an involuntary transfer to Nondalton, behaved as though he not-so-secretly harbored a grudge against every teacher under his authority.

His attitude and resulting behavior baffled me, especially when he singled me out as one of the recipients of his vile nature, because I'd never even encountered the man until that point in my life. I spent a good deal of my time attempting to sidestep his miserably vindictive personality.

Chigmit Mountains near Nondalton.

The fact that I worked under the immediate supervision of the Director of Special Education for our region did little to smooth the waters in my relations with Principal Bartlett. If anything, that little fact simply exacerbated the enmity directed at me. He and the principal had a tumultuous relationship and I was caught in the middle.

Rather than become embroiled in Bartlett's constant warfare with the Special Education Director, I tried to remove myself from the fray, endeavoring instead to focus on my students and their varying academic needs. That attitude probably kept me out of a goodly number of the conflicts that arose at the school, but not all of them.

———

I truly enjoyed the residents of the village and their children. My Special Education students posed numerous challenges on a daily basis, but even the most fractious of the children sensed my fondness for them.

My students responded well to kindness and consistency, and they slowly began to display growing personal confidence and modest scholastic achievements under my tutelage. As a reward for their efforts, I held a monthly party at the school. We delighted in watching videos, played a variety of board games, and munched popcorn during those Saturday afternoon social gatherings.

Although I made every effort to avoid the personality conflicts that arose at school, primarily with the principal, I found myself embroiled in periodic battles that took a toll on my overall emotional and physical health. I confided my upset during a conversation with Carrie, the school district's traveling guidance counselor, and she reassured me that I wasn't guilty of imagining or provoking the stress I was experiencing. She even offered me pointers on ways of dealing with the principal.

The stress worsened, however, as did my symptoms. Finally, I was forced to travel to Anchorage on emergency leave in order to see a doctor for a check-up. The doctor declared that my physical ailments were, indeed, stress-induced, and he subsequently reported his findings to the Director of Special Education.

As far as the Special Education Director was concerned, Principal Bartlett was culpable, because he'd targeted me in his constant wars with the Special Education division of the school district.

The Director made his feelings known to Bartlett's superior, who apparently instructed the principal to clean up his act and mind his manners where I was concerned.

Also, the Director advised me to keep a journal account of all of my dealings with Principal Bartlett. I agreed with his conclusion that I might need this written record for later reference should a school district hearing ever be necessary. I kept the journal hidden, not willing to risk an unannounced visit to my trailer by the principal, and his subsequent discovery of my recorded account of each school day and my encounters with him.

Believe me when I tell you that, although I had few illusions, I was very relieved by the temporary cessation of overt hostility and stinging comments by the principal. However, I didn't expect it to last forever. And, it didn't.

———

Transportation by air into and out of Nondalton truly unnerved me, especially when shortcuts through the very narrow, often foggy, and invariably turbulent air of Lake Clark Pass occurred.

Although the Lake Clark Pass route was a shorter alternative to normal air travel, which required a route over the mountains and much more fuel, it was a terrorizing ride for the passengers. I knew the history of the aviation accidents that had taken place in the Lake Clark Pass, and that simply contributed to my heightened anxiety levels.

The pilots attempted to reassure me whenever I was on board, but their words fell on deaf ears as I stared, heart lodged in my throat, at the mountainous terrain that rose on either side of the aircraft like towering sentinels of doom. A quick glance out the window told me that the tips of the plane's wings were mere inches from the frozen walls of that pass and the promise of a crash was just a heartbeat away from becoming reality.

Powerful crosswinds often prevented landings on Nondalton's airstrip. I was aboard an aircraft that wound up executing "touch and go's" on the runway as the pilot repeatedly attempted to land the plane. As an alternative to these failed efforts, the frustrated pilot then attempted to land on the frozen lake surface. That wasn't meant to be, either.

We wound up flying on to Iliamna, a nearby village, and landing there, then taking ground transportation for the final leg of the journey into Nondalton. Our transportation that day was an ambulance. The ultimate irony! I decided.

I might have endured that particular ordeal, but it aged me ten years in the space of an hour. And quite some time passed before I was willing to risk a flight to Anchorage again.

———

Christmas in Nondalton was a subdued and somewhat lonely affair that year. Not being a part of an established social group at the school, I expected to celebrate Christmas on my own. My plan was to relax and rest at home, a not altogether bad idea once I looked out the window and saw the blizzard brewing in the distant skies.

In the end, though, my classroom aide persuaded me to join her and her family at her home for Christmas dinner. She drove her snowmobile to my trailer and collected me for the ride back to her house. I must admit that it was quite a unique experience to be fed fish-eye soup, a very popular Native dish, rather than the traditional turkey and stuffing meal I generally associate with the Christmas holidays.

———

Aside from the predictable upsets caused by the principal, the school year unfolded with its usual academic routine and rhythm. By the summer months, I was relieved to be able to return to Anchorage for a much-needed break from all of the bickering among the teachers and the escalating tension because of Principal Bartlett.

Surprisingly, my Nondalton teaching contract was renewed for the next school year, but this was more the result of an excellent Teacher Evaluation from the Director of Special Education than from any positive comments made on my behalf by the principal. I had mixed feelings about returning to Nondalton, but in the end I concluded that I could tolerate Principal Bartlett for one more year.

———

Since tenants occupied my Anchorage house, I house-sat for an acquaintance for part of the summer. I also visited an old friend in British Columbia, flying into Vancouver and then traveling by bus to Nanaimo, where my friend welcomed me. We completed the final leg of the journey to her island home aboard a Zodiac, a small rubber inflatable that bobbed like a cork atop the tumultuous waves.

I didn't stay long on the island. My host had been hospitalized with pneumonia. His wife, a very old friend, was preoccupied with her husband's impending surgery and not in a good frame of mind for a houseguest, so I cut short my visit and returned to Alaska.

I knew I needed to meet the academic requirement that summer of six college-level credit hours in Early Childhood/Special Education classes because I was teaching pre-school children. The School District, as well as the Director of Special Education, had made this course work a condition of my return to teaching in September.

I immediately enrolled at the University of Alaska, attending classes, conducting sample testing, and listening to lectures by various authorities. The instructor for the classes left a great deal to be desired, but most of the students weathered her inconsistency and somewhat off-the-wall emphasis on study areas that had nothing to do with our Special Education teaching. I met the requirements, passing my final exams just hours before I departed for Oregon.

I rented a two-story beach house situated at the edge of the ocean for a month-long vacation. I invited an old friend to share my vacation lodgings, and he occupied the downstairs apartment.

At the start of the school year, I returned to Nondalton. Sadly, more of the same conflict with Principal Bartlett awaited me. If anything, the man had grown more irrational since the close of school the previous year.

I was nervous whenever the principal was in close proximity to my students and me. His wife, an equally irascible creature, exacerbated the fire already raging in the man's psyche. Their arguments, too embarrassing for words if one witnessed them, became the stuff of legends at our school.

As my frustration mounted during the school year, I finally felt that I had no other alternative but to report my difficulties with Principal Bartlett to the Alaska State Teachers' Union. They dispatched a representative to interview all of the parties involved in the dilemma. Then, the union representative presented his recommendations for a truce to an enraged Bartlett.

When a principal and his teachers fail to achieve a harmonious relationship, everyone—from students to teachers to support personnel—suffers. No one is exempt from the conflict or the stress that is generated, and the school year becomes a never-ending endurance test for everyone.

The singular blessing for me during that final Nondalton year was my students. Saying farewell to the children at the end of school is always difficult, but even more so when you realize that they are often victims of adults gone awry—adults like their school principal, who disciplined them by humiliating them in front of the other students and who had an unerring instinct for compounding their Special Education status with comments guaranteed to diminish their self-esteem.

Nondalton students.

I grew close to several of my Special Education students, often entertaining them in my trailer on the weekends and supervising them during various extracurricular activities when classes ended each day. I've also stayed in contact with some of them.

I eventually learned through the teacher gossip grapevine that Principal Bartlett accepted a position as a School Superintendent in another town, but caused so many conflicts in the school district and among the teachers under his supervision, he was finally terminated with cause. Bartlett and his long-suffering wife eventually departed Alaska, much to everyone's relief, I'm sure.

"Life is to be lived. If you have to support yourself, you had bloody well better find some way that is going to be interesting. And you don't do that by sitting around wondering about yourself."

Katharine Hepburn

Twenty-Six

I sold my little house and bought a dream home that I had driven by and watched for ten years. By this time I had saved enough for a down payment and the house was now mine.

There were trees in the back yard and the front was covered with wild flowers and more trees. A glass atrium, two bedrooms, library, two bathrooms, two car-garage, paneled rooms, cathedral ceilings, and a gas fireplace was now my home.

I returned to Anchorage to settle into my new address, buying furniture and getting my possessions from storage.

I truly savored the resumption of a non-Bush life and the beginning of what I assumed was my retirement from teaching.

While a broadening and often enriching personal experience, Bush village teaching is both difficult and worthwhile. Teaching at the "Top of the World" had translated into makeshift accommodations, honey buckets, hand carrying my own water supplies, doing without proper dietary items like fresh fruits and vegetables, and feeling like an itinerant worker.

I loved the people of the villages and towns in which I taught. I also had achieved my long sought after goal of financial security, which would allow me to retire and live independently without the stress of wondering if I could keep a roof over my own head.

With the benefit of hindsight, I'm certain that the children enabled me to tolerate the multiple environmental miseries and the small-minded personalities I encountered during those years. In fact, the children inspire me to this day. They provided my life with the kind of purpose I might otherwise have never attained had I pursued any other profession.

In 1996, I'd been retired for almost a year. To be quite candid, I was constantly bored. When the Superintendent of the Kuspuk School District telephoned and asked me to consider a position as a substitute teacher at Crooked Creek, I was excited about the prospect of getting back into the classroom.

After I told her that I would accept her invitation, she surprised me by saying, "Would you consider taking on a permanent teaching position?"

Her question should have set off an alarm in my head, warning me that all was not well in Crooked Creek. Alas, no alarm sounded, and I agreed to accept employment on a temporary basis. I decided it would be best to wait to determine if a full-time, permanent position would suit my future needs. Had I signed a contract and then resigned, I would have made myself vulnerable to a school district lawsuit for breach of contract as a result of a premature withdrawal from the commitment.

A haste-filled departure from Anchorage, which seems to be my karma, followed the Superintendent's phone call and my subsequent acceptance of her offer. Within two days I was on an airplane. After landing in Aniak, I boarded a small private plane for the final fifty miles to Crooked Creek. The majority of my possessions, which I'd shipped in large boxes via parcel post at the post office in Anchorage, would eventually arrive.

———

Crooked Creek is a tiny Bush village with a population of about one hundred people. Two hundred and seventy-five miles west of Anchorage, it is situated in the Kilbuk-Kuskokwim Mountains.

With an average snowfall of eight-five to ninety inches, the winter temperatures sink as low as minus fifty-nine degrees. In stark contrast, the summer temperatures can climb into the plus ninety-degree range.

My spirits fell when I caught my first glimpse of the dilapidated village of Crooked Creek. It was little more than a jumble of weathered old structures, all badly in need of repair, a post office, a general store that charged exorbitant prices, and the school in which I would teach.

The principal of the school met me when I arrived, the first words out of his mouth an apology for my prospective accommodations. I'd lived in some fairly undesirable places as a Bush teacher, and I told myself that I could handle just about any living situation.

However, even I was horrified when we arrived at the dwelling he called "The Cave." My new home was ten steps down from a toxic waste facility.

The bedroom and living room contained the filthiest wreckage of alleged furniture that I'd ever seen in my entire life. The extra bedroom was home to stacks of stored lumber. Why store lumber in the spare bedroom of a residence? I haven't a clue!

Holes in the floors, sealed over with duct tape, promised a broken leg if one took a wrong step and crashed through the rotting wood. The bathroom was in such wretched condition, I gagged when I walked into it. The shower and toilet were black from rusty water. If you made the mistake of flushing the toilet, the sewage spewed up into the shower stall, the latter facility unusable thanks to the accumulated grime and grunge.

Exposed wiring, holes in the walls with clumps of asbestos-tainted insulation spilling out, and a sagging ceiling completed the interior tour of the hovel in which I was expected to live.

Abandoned equipment, discarded piles of rotting garbage, pools of sewage, and miscellaneous trash of every possible description littered the exterior area surrounding the house. Now, here's the real shocker—I was expected to pay the outrageous sum of $560, plus utilities, for monthly rental on this nightmare.

No wonder the previous teacher, who'd departed after exactly one day on the job, had left so quickly. If I'd had any sense, I would have immediately fled Crooked Creek, too, but I've always been too stubborn and too determined for my own good.

My outrage over the condition of the shack the school district expected me to inhabit resulted in my receiving permission to live and work in the trailer that housed my classroom on the school's campus. I telephoned constantly to complain about my housing situation. The Superintendent caved under the pressure of my persistence, but only temporarily, as it turned out.

Although not very clean—I wore rubber boots in the shower and scrubbed it as best I could—the school shower was an improvement over the one at my "house." I also stored my perishable food in the school's cafeteria refrigerator, much to the annoyance of the school cook.

There were four other teachers at the school in Crooked Creek. Winston, my favorite of all of my colleagues, was a good-natured African-American man whose wife and two children had left the village because of the intolerable living conditions. Winston's mother, upon seeing a photograph of Winston Churchill hanging on the wall following her son's birth, announced, "I want to name my son after him." Winston was fortunate that the photo wasn't of Hitler or Mussolini.

Originally from a small Native Alaska community and accus-

Students in class at Crooked Creek.

tomed to a humbler lifestyle, even Winston's wife couldn't handle, let alone improve, the living conditions. Winston paid an additional $100 each month because his dwelling possessed a front and a back porch. Never mind the fact that the windows facing out onto the porch were broken, and Winston had stuffed them with cardboard and newspaper to cut down on the drafts from the bitterly cold arctic air.

———

My fifteen Crooked Creek students were energetic and enthusiastic children. They possessed an almost tangible desire to learn, so our time together in the classroom each day passed at lightning speed. It was those nights I spent on a cot in the unheated classroom that challenged my dedication as a teacher.

When the school district's Superintendent visited me a few weeks after my arrival, I was informed that I couldn't use my classroom as a place to sleep at night. Being forbidden to sleep and bathe at the school ended whatever patience with or loyalty to the school district that I might have felt during my early days in Crooked Creek. And, thanks to the fact that I hadn't signed a contract with the district, I was able to leave.

Although I deeply regretted leaving my students, I knew that I had no other choice. I turned in my notice, announcing my intention to immediately end my commitment as a teacher to the Crooked Creek students.

I'd endured three weeks in hell, and I was unwilling to continue. I'd already paid for my own transportation to the village, and I'd spent a considerable sum of money on non-perishable food supplies. Further financial losses weren't acceptable.

———

Prior to my departure from Crooked Creek in 1997, the acting principal gave me a flyer about a Special Education teacher opening in another school district. When I inquired about the position, I received the news that I was over-qualified. *There's a first time for everything!* I thought.

The Superintendent for the Alaska Gateway School District then proceeded to offer me an alternative position with a fair salary—a combination Assistant Superintendent and Special Education teacher.

Although I admitted that I didn't possess budgetary, administrative, or grant writing experience, and despite the fact that several other more qualified individuals were interviewed for the position, I was still considered the best candidate for the job because of my Special Education experience and certification.

I accepted!

Twenty-Seven

Tok is the home of the Alaska Gateway School District, which serves the needs of seven individual schools—Dot Lake, Eagle, Mentasta, Tanacross, Tetlin, Tok, and Northway.

According to local legend, the name Tok came from the husky pup that had been the mascot of the U.S. Army's 97th Engineer Corps, which was made up of primarily black soldiers, during the building of the Alaska Highway. Reputedly the "Dog Sled Capitol of Alaska," dog sled races and competitions are held all winter long.

Tok Cutoff affords anyone driving a vehicle the choice of taking the Alaska Highway the two hundred and five miles to Fairbanks or the three hundred and thirty mile route to Anchorage. I note this as a point of interest, because I'd spent so many years in Bush villages where one had to utilize aircraft transportation in order to travel into or out of the community.

Living in Tok made personal travel much easier, as well as far more economical without the cost of airfare. Despite the distance, I frequently drove to Anchorage on weekends. I also explored the Fairbanks area and Whitehorse in the Northwest Territories for much needed changes of scenery, the luxury of traveling by car was one I savored.

Tok was home to about fifteen hundred people. It was also the commercial center for several nearby villages. Since Tok was not incorporated, the residents didn't pay the "city" for snow removal, the education of their children, or garbage removal. The first community of any size upon entering Alaska from Canada, Tok is just ninety three miles from the border.

The winter months in Tok are extremely cold, the temperatures generally hovering around minus thirty-two degrees, if you don't consider the wind chill factor. In order to keep your car in working order, it's necessary to provide a source of heat that will keep the engine block and radiator from freezing and cracking. Summer is very pleasant and mild, with the average temperature generally in the low seventies.

There were gift shops, grocery stores, hardware store, post office, medical clinic, restaurants, library, Visitor's Information Center, both elementary and high schools, and a university extension facility in Tok. All of these establishments are an advantage to anyone who has lived in the Bush and been deprived of these conveniences for months on end.

—

Arriving in 1997, I rented half of a modest duplex from a teacher's aide who worked at the Tok Elementary School. Unlike my previous abode in Crooked Creek, this dwelling possessed reasonable furnishings, a functional kitchen, proper plumbing, untainted water, and a roof that wasn't on the verge of falling in on my head.

My landlady allowed me the use of her washer and dryer. She also invited me over for coffee and conversation every once in a while. I think it's fair to say that we became comfortable acquaintances during my time in Tok.

Although she grilled me upon occasion, I avoided gossip about the school district with my landlady. Her work as a teacher's aide persuaded me that she could easily become a source of information among the various teachers in town and, as her source, I could easily come to the attention of my superiors in a less than desirable manner. As it was, I already felt inadequate in my job.

———·———

I do not have much experience in administration. I admit that fact of my life without hesitation or remorse, especially since I readily confessed to this reality when I interviewed for the position with the Alaska Gateway School District's Superintendent.

Without any of the experience necessary for the work for which I'd been hired, I was soon made the Director of Special Programs for the school district and supervisor to seven employees. Why? Your guess is as good as mine.

With grant application forms due in short order, I searched for samples of previously written and funded grants so that I could use a successful model. A teacher in the school district took pity on me when he saw my panic over the current state of affairs, and guided me through the process of writing the first grant. I remain in his debt for his kindness and assistance.

———·———

My work at the Alaska Gateway School District involved a wide variety of tasks, including personnel evaluations, creating the budget, ordering curriculum and project materials, making on-site school visits, and developing in-service training programs for the teachers. I also prepared school calendars, helped the principals establish goals for their teachers and students, and, my all-time favorite task, worked with Special Education students when visiting the various schools.

The demands of my job were varied and the hours extremely long that year. When I departed at the end of the school year, I did so with a clear conscience. I'd been hurled into a sink-or-swim situation, done my best, and survived the experience.

As well, my salary that year and the sale of my first home in Anchorage afforded me the opportunity to pay off the mortgage on the second home I'd purchased during my years of teaching in the Bush.

Epilogue

It will not surprise you, I'm sure, that the most gratifying aspect of my Alaskan odyssey involved the many children for whom I was responsible as a teacher. I felt a devotion to all my students, and a reciprocal devotion from many of them, that is very difficult to describe. Suffice to say, my emotions were always engaged with those kids.

My students were an eternal blessing and a constant challenge. They were the reason I got out of bed every morning despite the brutal weather conditions and the often uninhabitable dwellings I occupied.

They constantly stimulated my intellect, they aroused my protective instincts, and they gifted me with their trust. And, in a more poignant way, they allowed me the pleasure of expressing the more nurturing maternal side of my personality.

I may be retired from teaching, but I still think often of my former students. I hear from many of them.

Although my teaching career came to a close when I retired, I like to think that I made a difference in the lives of some of my students. I also hope that they will remember me with the same love that I will always feel for them.

Life lesson: Lead with your heart.

On a final note, I think my students would be delighted to learn that I married the love of my life after I retired from teaching. Steve is my soul-mate, and I credit him as the inspiration for this book.

"It's only when we truly know and understand that we have a limited time on earth—and that we have no way of knowing when our time is up—that we will begin to live each day to the fullest, as if it was the only one we had."

Elizabeth Kubler-Ross